BATTLE FOR GEMSTONES

SAKSHI PAREEK

Published by InkQuills Publishing House
www.inkquills.in

First Edition 2023

ISBN: 978-93-90567-44-7

This book is completely dedicated to the spiritual power following me, protecting me, guiding me and loving me throughout my life!

ACKNOWLEDGEMENTS

Words and a page would be less when it comes to thanking and acknowledging people who played their role in making this dream possible. Still, let me try.

Above all, let me, first of all, thank the spiritual power that has been following me, guiding me, and loving me throughout my life. Nothing is above that. I am breathing, walking and talking, doing every little stuff because of that.

After that, I would like to mention my father here. I'm very sure that no father in the world could ever love his daughter, the way my father does. His love is beyond this mortal world. Whatever I am capable of doing involves a great part of his love and blessings.

Coming next, my mother, my younger brother, and my sister are three more persons in my life who can never be thanked enough for loving me unconditionally. The faith and trust that my family has in me are beyond one's imagination.

My in-laws including my father-in-law, mother-in-law, and sister-in-law have been the most amazing in-laws one could ever ask for. I'm able to put this book into your hand with their love and support as well.

It will be an injustice if I will mention a few names of my friends here. This is because I am blessed with countless friends and well-wishers who are always there in my life to love me and support me. Let me thank them all here.

How can I not mention my husband here? Words are less to thank him enough for the love and support he displays for me

24*7. He always wanted me to be a career-oriented woman. I have come this far with his support only.

Last, but not least, let me thank Abhisar Garg, founder of InkQuills Publishing House for having trust in my work. He has always been a dear friend more than just a publisher for me. I would say that he is the sole reason this book came into literary world.

A special thanks to both my maternal and paternal grandmothers.

Contents

1

The Coronet

Princess Aarunya was gazing at the gemstones in the coronet for over a minute now. Her big beautiful eyes were persistently looking at the coronet. It was attractive and alluring. It wasn't an ordinary coronet that any king or prince would wear on their heads. It was rather big and different than any other coronet. Its allure was extraordinary and uncommon because of the gemstones it had embedded. With four big colourful gemstones on its surface, it could win anyone's eyes. Aarunya was a princess of seventeen and her obsession toward the coronet was little unusual. Although the shine of gemstones was touching every corner of the room, that light found most of the attention in Aarunya's eyes.

Among the four colourful gemstones, the yellow gem was dazzling in her eyes. Indubitably, the yellow gem was the brightest gem among all. Though Aarunya's eyes were gazing all the gemstones in the coronet with love but it was the yellow stone that captured her heart. The allure of blue was none less than the yellow. It contained its own brightness within, it was different than yellow. The major difference between yellow and blue gem was that the blue one was bright but still carried its noticeable serenity. Yellow, on the other hand, was brightest and powerfully glistening.

The gleam of those sleeping gemstones made Aarunya think and question herself, how beautiful they will look if they are awakened. Red gem on the coronet wasn't pleasing to eyes like the others, as its colour was striking the eyes and wasn't soothing. But it was evident that it is as powerful as the others and its quest is to gain more power than it already has. Then there came the last gem, the green one. The glow of the green gem was also attractive and alluring, but prominently it was less than the others. Its uniqueness was its soothing and calm presence as compared to other gems. Green gem had its own uniqueness and tranquillity. Behind the coronet there was a transparent gem, which Aarunya didn't like and never cared about. Even the books she had about gemstones have nothing to say about the transparent gemstone. This is the reason; she didn't like it much. She presumed it to be powerless.

Aarunya was holding the coronet in her hand since long. In a highly luxurious room of the palace, she was standing alone. Her attire reflected her status, the royal princess of the fourteenth century. Though she was a daughter of Brahmin emperor, still the gleam of her face was none less than any Rajput or Kshatriya princess of those times. Very less princely states were ruled by Brahmins, and one among them was Krishnapur. Located in the middle of India, it was flourished with food crops, grains, and rivers to add into the affirmative points. It was considered a wealthy nation among the Brahmin estates. Even the other Rajput estates envied the flourishment and nourishment of Krishnapur. Aarunya was the proud daughter of the then king Mahendra. King had one daughter and one son, Aarav.

It was visible on Aarunya's face that she was obsessed with the coronet and gemstones. She was staring at it like a young girl would stare in her lover's eyes. When Aarunya was busy staring the coronet, one of her servants disturbed her in her thoughts and said, "Your Highness! The Queen is coming to see you." Aarunya hesitated when she found that her servant might have seen her obsessing with the coronet. She hide it behind her golden dupatta and replied, "Alright! I am waiting for her." She wanted to stare at gems for a long time but this time none but her own mother, the queen of Krishnapur, had disturbed her.

Soon her mother walked into the room. "Mother," she uttered. The word, 'Mother,' from her mouth was more of a question enquiring about her purpose of the visit than a salutation. Queen's appearance was none less than young princess Aarunya. Anyone could tell that they were mother and daughter in just one look. She was holding her beauty in her late thirties, with all grace. Aarunya had acquired all her beauty traits and glow on her face from her mother.

Queen saw the coronet in her hand, she was trying to hide it even from the queen. "Aarunya," queen called her name. Queen's tone of calling her name specified that she was asking her what she is hiding from her. Queen's eyes were on her hand which was hiding the coronet. There was no sense in hiding the coronet from her. She took it in front of her and said, "Soon, father will awaken the gemstones, see them, how glorious they are, aren't they?" she asked. Aarunya first tried to hide the coronet from queen, when she was unsuccessful, she became unabashed and started the conversation praising the coronet. Queen kept quiet, she didn't even look at the coronet. She was persistently gazing her daughter, who was holding the coronet. It was clear that the queen was not obsessed with the coronet like Aarunya. The mother and daughter who although had similar looks, had different personalities altogether.

After a pause, Aarunya said, "Mother, the yellow is the most powerful one among them. See its alluring light, I just can't take my eyes of it. I can keep looking at it for an eternity." While speaking, Aarunya's eyes were focussed on the yellow gem. Queen was still silent; she didn't respond to her about the beauty of the coronet or the yellow gem. Aarunya didn't care about her response. She was so lost in the beauty and power of the coronet and its gemstones. She continued, "The blue one is equally pretty. It attracts me like the big blue sky and all the blue oceans of the world. Its beauty is irresistible. Mother, yellow is powerful and the blue is consuming me." Queen closed her eyes and twisted her eyebrows, clearly, she didn't favour her daughter's obsession with the coronet. The way the queen closed her eyes showed how her daughter's obsession with the coronet and gemstones distressed her.

Aarunya still didn't notice her mother's disregard in hearing the praises for the coronet and the gemstones. She added, "Mother do you know, what's the best thing about the red gem? Its beauty says that the one who'll hold this will have irresistible hunger of power. The light that it emits wants more and more. At the moment it is less than the yellow and blue, but its urge to gain more and more, makes it perfect." When she was done speaking about the red, she looked at her mother, who was sitting like a numb idol, who can't speak and move.

"Aren't you excited to wear these as rings? Aren't you excited when father and brother Aarav will bring that girl who'll help us awaken these gemstones, we all will save our ancestors," she referred to the purpose of awakening the gemstones, the first time since she had starting talking about the coronet. She mentioned that her father and brother have gone outside to bring one girl to awaken the gemstones. They ought to awaken the gemstones for saving the ancestors.

"Is that all you want?" Queen asked, looking in her eyes. "Yes mom, I want ancestors to be saved, as soon as possible," she replied with little confidence. So, the gemstones need to be awakened to save ancestors, but that's not all that Aarunya wants, she wants to hold one of those magical and powerful gemstones as a ring in her hand. "Check yourself, aren't you obsessed with the power of gemstones," the queen asked again. Queen wanted her consent in the fact that more than saving the ancestors, her urge is to hold the power of gemstones is more. "*For me, the obsession towards power is like breathing,*" she replied. Her mother's facial expression worsened after hearing that. Looking at her, Aarunya added, "And certainly you deserve the green gem, dull than the others and boring too." She depicted from her words that among the gemstones, she liked the green gem the least. She also meant that she was distributing four gemstones among her four family members, according to their personality and traits.

After a pause, she added, "My goal is selfless too, I wish to wear them for the sake of our ancestors." Queen distressed with her statement. Her facial expressions were saying it all. "I doubt," queen said. Aarunya twisted her lips, blinked her eyes and replied, "Well, then maybe you are right. I crave the power that every gem holds within, and I am excited to wear one of them in my finger. Undoubtedly, I'll ask father to give me the yellow one. It's the most powerful and amazing among all." In just another sentence she accepted her obsession for the gemstones and mostly towards the yellow one.

"How you are so sure that yellow is most powerful among them?" Queen asked about Aarunya's inferences. "Books, mother…books. Books that grandmother gave me. I have spent my seventeen years' life, reading the books about gemstones. It says that the green gain its power from the plants of the earth, red being the element of the blood of humans has energy of a human as its source. Blue gain its power from the water and the yellow one, the yellow one gains the power from… the sun." She said the word Sun with a peculiar lust and craving towards the gem. "Doesn't matter, you can only understand one book among them," said the queen. Queen added, "And even that book is half torned." Queen's words meant that there might be many books about gemstones and among them, Aarunya could understand only one book. She mocked on her abilities that she could understand only one book of gemstones and still she is mad after them.

She ignored and got up from the peacock shaped luxurious sofa she was sitting on. She was still holding the coronet. Gawking at the yellow gem, she continued to praise it, "Mother! Is there any doubt in your mind that the sun is most powerful among all?" Queen who was still sitting on the sofa said, "With that theory, you deserve the red one. A human who craves and lust for power." She smiled and replied, "Yes I am the human who craves and lust for power, and I wish to wear them all. But because I love all three of you, as equal to gemstones, therefore, I want you, brother and father too to wear them. I wish to wear just one of them, and I can do anything to wear one of it, one day, anything." She emphasised on the word anything. Her words said that even when she loves yellow the most, still she would happily wear any of those gemstones. Her words implied that her father, King Mahendra and Aarav will bring a girl who will awaken these gemstones and then all four of them will wear those gemstones as rings in their hands.

Queen was mentally tortured while seeing her only daughter's obsession with unnatural power. "What you and your father is doing is evil," said the queen. "Father is obsessed towards saving the ancestors, and I am obsessed towards the gemstones, our goals are maybe different but our destiny is same, and mother I promise you that soon we are going to achieve it, Soon." Aarunya's words had signs that she had great lust towards the power of gemstones.

"I just came here to ask you whether you have heard from your father because I haven't." The Queen finally told her the purpose of visiting her room. "Yes, father and brother have not reached Ratnagadh yet, and after reaching there, he'll be coming back to Krishnapur soon." "Alright," said the queen and left her alone again with the gemstones and coronet. She didn't spend any quality time with her daughter, in the absence of her husband and son.

Aarunya again began gazing the coronet and its beautiful gemstones. But again her obsession was disturbed by another of her servant. This servant entered without permission. She dared to do so because she was her friend. "Aarunya," she called her by her name. "What?" She replied in irritation, while looking at the coronet. She recognized her voice and this time she didn't bother to hide the coronet. Starring at coronet, dreaming about powers of gemstones, living in the virtual world of power and immortality, all these had become her favourite hobby. She never wanted to come out of it.

"If for a minute, you'll come out of this coronet and tales of gemstones then I'll tell you something more interesting than this," her friend said. She was still busy in analysing the enormous beauty of spectacular coronet and its gemstones. She didn't even shift her eyes from coronet to her friend to reply. "Nothing can be more interesting than this… nothing." Her voice carried a different kind of thirst towards those gemstones and their power. Her friend came near her and said in one breath, "You are so mad about these colourful stones, just because you have read about them in some stupid books. But what I'll tell you is all real, which is seen by eyes and heard by ears, not just read in books." Being her best friend only she could dare to say those words about the coronet, gemstones and the books on those gemstones.

Aarunya finally decided to do a favour for her friend, she shifted her eyes from her beloved coronet to her friend's face. "What on earth could be more special and interesting than my gemstones," she referred gemstones as hers with full confidence that one day she'll be the true owner of either all of them or certainly one of them. "How can you trust the books given by your grandmother so much that you are so mad about these gemstones." Her friend asked, before revealing about her interesting story, the one which she was referring more interesting than the gemstones.

Aarunya finally placed the coronet far from her hands, safe in her cupboard, maybe now she had decided to give some of her time to her friend. "My granny trusted no one else but me to give those books, not even my father. She gave it to me in her last moments. She was the most intelligent lady I had known in my entire life. These books cannot be wrong about gemstones, and neither can be my granny. I could read only one book, rest are in some foreign language, I can't understand them. The book that I understood says that these gemstones are sleeping and need to be awakened for gaining immortality and powers beyond imagination. Father will awaken these sleeping gemstones and will save ancestors from these gemstones, and then I'll use the power to become immortal and beautiful and young for the eternity," she exposed her thoughts about the book, gemstones and her dead granny. Those gemstones are a source of enormous power and immortality but why and how gemstones are to be awakened, why and how ancestors are to be saved, who are ancestors and from whom they need to be saved; Aarunya was unaware of all those questions. Maybe because she couldn't understand the other books about gemstones, given by her granny that's why she didn't know why and how gemstones need to be awakened, or maybe she had no interest in knowing anything except the fact of power and immortality in gemstones.

"What if I can fetch you that immortality without making efforts to awaken these gemstones," her friend said to sow the seeds of greed in her heart. "I hate jokes," she said to alarm her that she won't welcome jokes and pranks when it comes to those special gemstones. "I am not joking Aarunya, I have heard that behind the little hill of barista village, there is an old lady who can teach young girls, how to remain young and beautiful for eternity," she said with confidence in her voice. She was claiming that she can help Aarunya to walk to a lady who can teach her how to remain beautiful and young for eternity.

Aarunya laughed loudly on her words and said, "Do you know how ironical your words are. An old lady is teaching how to remain beautiful for eternity, if she was master in it, then how come she is old." Aarunya had logic and clarity in her thoughts. "Every soul living on this planet, craves for power," said Aarunya and added, "And so will that old lady. If she could make someone immortal, why won't she do that to herself." Her friend sighed and said, "Aarunya, for once believe my words, I have heard of her, from very secretive sources. That lady is said to be two hundred years old, and not every young girl can pass the test of becoming immortal and beautiful for eternity. If you want I can take you to meet her once, rest is your destiny." Plausibly Aarunya's friend was well aware of her greed of immortality and of remaining beautiful for eternity, this is because she was hitting her arches finely on her. She mentioned of passing some test for becoming immortal and beautiful for eternity.

Aarunya became conscious for once of her friend's words. She said, "Prove your words." She proclaimed like a queen to her and demanded to prove her words in her reality. Aarunya was in love with coronet and gemstones because they could fetch her immortality, power, and beauty for eternity. If anything else could give her the same then the gemstones would just reduce to colourful stones for her. "You just need to think, what you are going to say to the queen and definitely today in the night I'll take you there," said her friend. She asked her in words that moving out would require the queen's permission and for that Aarunya needs to be prepared. "I'll manage," she replied with confidence in her voice. She was sure that queen won't be an obstacle between anything, she can easily manage taking her consent. Aarunya was, after all, a princess of a well-reputed estate; moreover she was king's eye's apple. Taking all these things into consideration, she was in the habit of doing whatever her heart wants.

"But, there is one more condition," said her friend. "And…, what's that?" "We can only go there when the clock strikes 12, that old lady is supposed to come in that village's cemetery only in midnight," she explained. Aarunya's facial expressions changed in wonder. "What?" she cried in a jolt. Her shock was valid, as her friend talked of the cemetery and that too in midnight. Even after being the princess of a powerful realm, she was uncomfortable with doing some things, not because she was afraid but because what would happen if someone saw her there. Aarunya had already ignored the fact that her friend was asking her to go out to meet that lady in the night and now she was demanding to go to cemetery that too at midnight. This was enough for Aarunya to protest.

Aarunya's friend came near her. She lessened the distance and sat on the couch with full honour. Aarunya had given her that space. "Now, you can understand why every girl cannot become young and beautiful for eternity. This is because not every girl can dare to walk alone in a cemetery and that too in midnight," she added one more covenant. They need to go alone. "That means we can't even go with our soldiers," Aarunya asked the obvious question. "No, the old lady hates men," she replied. Aarunya's heart pondered whether she could do the asked act or not. She had few soldiers of her own, who are responsible for her safety, she could manage them easily to not to spit out the truth to anyone. But her friend wanted her not to take them along. She wondered for once that it would be a better option to wait for father to come and awaken those gemstones, to become immortal and young for eternity.

Aarunya wanted to go back into the tales of gemstones which were also promising her eternal beauty and young body, but then they were uncertain, and her friend was offering her an instant reward, the only thing she craved for in her entire life of seventeen years. This situation made Aarunya think about her friend's plan. "By the way, where you have heard of this old lady and her offerings," Aarunya finally got the senses to ask something sensible and obvious. "Why you are worried about that, don't you trust me, my sources are more accurate than your sources of tales of gemstones," she said. Aarunya being Aarunya trusted her words without any doubts. She didn't feel the need to ask her again about the sources from where her friend might have heard about the old lady and her capabilities.

"So when can we go?" Aarunya asked. This question of hers showed that she was interested in going and she has trusted her friend's words without demanding answers of why and how. Her greed of becoming immortal and beautiful for eternity was on its peak, and that made her forget about gemstones and look for another option. This was maybe because she had spent seventeen years thinking about immortality and eternal beauty. Her life was spent thinking about becoming immortal, so gradually she had become so mad that she would do anything to achieve what she wanted.

"I have heard that this process can only take place only when Sitara comet is visible in stars," her friend mentioned some astrological conditions. "Tonight is that night, and you are telling me about it in today's daytime," Aarunya complained. Aarunya in a second understood the astrological conditions and figured it out that today was the day when all those conditions will be fulfilled. She was given very less time to decide whether she should avail that option or not. "I can only tell about it when I'll come to know. Some secret messengers dropped me this message today. Tonight is the only option, else this night won't come in next twenty or thirty years," said her friend.

Aarunya started wondering what if the gemstones tales is proven wrong, then in next twenty to thirty years she'll become older than today and she won't be able to take benefits of this old lady's theory too. Her heart inclined towards a yes to the offer of her friend. But there were some other things, which were bothering her. "But father and brother are too not in the estate, how will the queen manage alone," Aarunya queried. "We'll return by tomorrow night, it's not a big deal." Aarunya was still in confusion whether she should go on or not. Her friend came near her, held her hand and said, "Trust me it will work." She agreed. "But my faith on gemstones is still unchanged, I still desire to hold them in the form of rings in my hand…," her friend cut her short and said, "In your eternally beautiful and young hand, don't you want that." She watered the sprouts of desires in her heart. She referred her hand to be young for forever, she was hitting again and again on her hidden desires. "Ok! Ask soldiers to company us only till the hill and then we'll proceed alone." Aarunya gave her the words of assurance. "No, first we'll visit my home which is nearby to the hill and then alone we'll proceed to the cemetery, else soldier's will doubt on us," Sahrindri suggested. There was no doubt that she was smarter than Aarunya. Aarunya replied, "Alright, that's fine. I'll say to the queen that we are visiting to see your sick mother." Aarunya planned what she is going to say to her mother about her visit to barista village.

Aarunya now had to take permission from the queen. That wasn't an easy task for her. It was not so that she believed on what her friend said blindly, but she wanted to see it by her eyes, for her own satisfaction. Her faith in the gemstone was still intact. She just wanted to see and test everything that might promise immortality and beauty for eternity.

She made her way to queen's room. The Queen was resting on her luxurious bed. No one was allowed to walk in to her room. Aarunya first decided to wait, till she wakes up, but then her impatient attitude got the best of her. After all, she needed to visit the old lady before the appearance of Sitara comet. "What's the matter?" Queen asked in surprise, as she wanted to know that what bothered her so much that Aarunya had disturb her in her sleep. Queen felt worried, as she thought that there might be something very serious and urgent, which Aarunya wanted to discuss.

"Mother, I want to go with Sahrindri to her village, her mother is sick," she referred to her friend's name and village. "What happened to her mother?" The queen asked in concern. "She is sick, since last one month and Sahrindri wants to see her, ever since she got married here, she had been serving to me very well, now I want to be with her when she needs me." Aarunya had craftily portrayed her words in front of her mother, so that she does not denies to her offer. Queen was a soft-hearted lady and Aarunya was aware of her mother's nature very well. She wanted to take full advantage of her mother's weakness.

"When do you want to go?" asked her mother. "Today only, we want to leave palace as soon as possible," Aarunya replied to ensure that she might get permission from her mother. She felt in her heart that she was getting late to visit the old lady in that village. "What, how is today possible, let your father and brother come, then one of them will accompany you," she said. "No, mother, we are already late, let us go today itself," she argued. "But how can you go alone, it won't be safe for a princess like you," her mother showed concern. "I am not a child mother, I'll take my soldiers with me, Sahrindri will be with me, I can take care of myself well." "Why can't you wait till your father and brother return," the queen asked. "What if her mother passes away by then," Aarunya tortured her mother emotionally. At last, her mother had to agree with her.

Aarunya and her friend Sahrindri left in no time. Queen stubbornly sent a lot of soldiers to company them in their way. Barista village was not far from Krishnapur. While they were getting ready to leave, the queen was, again and again, asking the princess to take care of herself. She insisted even on accompanying them but Aarunya denied her saying that someone should be there to take care of the palace and pupils.

Queen sent enough soldiers to take care of them. They headed to barista village. Sahrindri was guiding them on the way. They reached her village by night. The troop rested in Sahrindri's house. Aarunya was guiding her soldiers to move, according to the guidance of Sahrindri. Sahrindri and Aarunya acted to meet her mother in front of the troop of soldiers.

At the night time, Sahrindri was serving dinner to the troop. Every soldier was traumatized to notice that their queen was eating with them. Aarunya had treated Sahrindri like her little sister, so she had no shame in having dinner at her room. Unlike her palace, there was no luxury at her home. Though Sahrindri was trying her best to make her feel special but her efforts were a pinch of salt in dish made for hundreds of people. But Aarunya didn't let her feel that she is her queen and Sahrindri is her servant. She ate food with all simplicity.

After the dinner was over, Sahrindri was busy in the kitchen. Aarunya went in and whispered in her ear, "When and how we'll go to the cemetery?" Sahrindri noticed her quest and enthusiasm to go to the cemetery that night. She, at first, smirked, listening to her question. Aarunya was worried about the visibility of Sitara comet. "Soon after the soldiers fall asleep, we'll change our clothes and will head to the hill," said Sahrindri. Excitement and impatient attitude was visible on Aarunya's face.

Soon after the soldiers fell asleep, the ladies changed their clothes. It was necessary that no one notices Aarunya in the village in her royal attire. It was midnight, Aarunya was little terrified to walk alone with her friend, behind the hill of barista village, but her desires persuaded her to do so. Like thieves, they were walking in the woods. It was night time; the light of the moon made it creepier than anything else.

They kept moving in between the woods. The breeze of night was blowing at its normal pace, but that night it seemed stronger than usual. Moonlight on the woods and leaves made them look like fireflies near the fire. Everywhere it was dark, the deep forest was opening its arms more deeply into a never-ending way. "How do you know the exact way Sahrindri?" Aarunya asked. Though it was Sahrindri's village, but the way towards the hill was extremely difficult. It was all dark in woods of forest. Her question was all fine that how she came to know about this difficult way, in just one day. "I have lived first fifteen years of my life here.," she explained her.

"Now we just need to cross this small hill," said Sahrindri while pointing out the small visible hill. Though the hill was really small and easy to climb but that was really a tough roadmap for the princess who wasn't in the habit of walking even half a mile. Princess today had already covered the distance of more than three kilometers on her feet, and now Sahrindri was asking her to climb a small hill.

She sat on a rock and said, "I am already tired Sahrindri, I need some rest." She was panting and breathing heavily. She had been raised in beds of flowers, how could she cross the path of thrones in just one day. "Princess, we are short of time, Sitara comet will be visible in just half an hour, and it will be there in the sky for next half an hour. We have to reach there on time and come back home too before morning's sunshine." Sahrindri showed her part of concern.

Aarunya got up to walk with her. Though she was panting and breathing heavily but her endless desires of becoming eternally beautiful were pursuing her to cross every path of difficulty that came before her. With heavy breaths and fast heartbeats, they started crossing the hill. Even Sahrindri got tired after a while. "Don't we have water with us?" asked Aarunya, as she had the habit of carrying all comforts and needs with her while travelling. "No, I was specially told not to carry water or any sort of comforts with us while coming here," Sahrindri replied. "Who refused you this specially," Aarunya asked in wonder. For once Sahrindri's face's colour changed, and she panicked, it seemed that she had spit out something which she shouldn't have spoken.

"The sources which bought you and I here," she replied after a while. "What are the sources, why aren't you telling me anything about the sources," Aarunya asked while they were moving downside the hill. "What you are worried about, the sources or about becoming eternally beautiful," Sahrindri tried to close the matter again. "Don't you want to become beautiful for eternity," Aarunya asked the perfect question, as Sahrindri had been helping her to become eternally beautiful then she might want the same thing for herself also. "I cannot accomplish the tasks which are required to become so," she replied. "Then how can I accomplish those," Aarunya asked again. "You'll know soon because we have reached," she replied and pointed towards a small hut where the old lady must be waiting for them. "Have we crossed cemetery?" Aarunya asked. "We are standing in between the cemetery," Sahrindri replied. Then Aarunya noticed the nearby surroundings. They were really standing in the cemetery. Her heartbeats went faster when she felt the terror of standing in such a negative place. But every time she felt anything negative, her desires would overrule her pessimism about the happenings of that night.

Under the moonlight, there were same dark trees and breeze was blowing on its pace. Moonlight was serving only to add into the horrible scenario of the moment. The hut was visible, only one little candle was lightened in the hut. Aarunya was no doubt petrified to enter that hut. Sahrindri took her hand and they proceeded to move inside the hut.

While holding each other's hand, they proceeded towards the hut. When they moved in, Aarunya saw an old, creepy lady was sleeping on the floor. Her wrinkles made her look terrible like a witch. She was wearing a white saree. Aarunya thought that she might be a widow. "So the girl with gemstones has come to my hut," she uttered while sleeping. Aarunya's jaw dropped when she heard the word gemstones from old lady's mouth. Her terror vanished in seconds as her obsession towards the gem hasn't gone yet.

"How does she know that I have gemstones, this is the truth only a few people know, which includes you and my entire family," she asked while looking in the eyes of Sahrindri. "I don't know Aarunya," she replied in trembling voice. "I know everything Aarunya, I even know that you both have lied about

Sahrindri's mother's sickness to the queen," said the old lady. She seemed a perfect witch, the one who knows everything about you and the one can perform all dark magic.

"How do you know all of this and what you want from us?" Aarunya said in the tone of an estate's princess. Now she was worried about the safety of her gemstones. She had spent years loving those gemstones, how could she forget them in promises of an old lady, whom she had met a few minutes ago. "That is not important, important is how to awaken those gemstones, don't you think so?" the old lady added. The old lady was even aware of the fact of awakening the gemstones. "My father and brother will do that task," she said with pride and confidence on her brother and father. "But your brother and father are not in estate, and they are too far from here, how you are going to protect your gemstones then?" the old lady asked. She tried to panic her.

Aarunya wasn't happy with her questions, after all she was the princess and she wanted the tasks to be accomplished on time and order. "I am here, because I have heard you can make young girls beautiful for eternity, your job is to do that, not to ask questions, which aren't your concern," Aarunya commended in her bold voice of a princess. She was, however, wondering in her mind that how come the old lady knows so much about gemstones and her family.

The old lady got up, took her stick and came near Aarunya. By now only half of her face was visible and she looked horrible in that, when she came near her, her full face was scarier and creepier than before. Her broken teeth were adding to the ugliness of her face. She whispered, "I can give you endless powers to protect your gemstones, you will need them soon. Not only you'll become immortal and eternally beautiful but also you'll become powerful enough to fight with an entire army to protect your gemstones and you'll need that." "But why would I need to fight from any army," Aarunya asked. "Because I am forecasting that soon your estate will face an attack from another strong estate in the absence of your father and brother," old lady replied. Aarunya's heart was scared hearing about the attack. But for then, the only important thing for Aarunya was to become immortal and perpetually beautiful.

"But if she'll be eternally beautiful and powerful then why will she need gemstones?" Sahrindri asked. While Aarunya was lost in the worry of attack on estate, in the absence of her father and brother. "Power is a lust, with awakened gemstones she'll become powerful, more than any other creature of the world, then why wouldn't she want those," said the old lady. A smile came on Aarunya's face, imagining about the immense power she'll be holding with the help of old lady. "Are you sure about the attack?" she asked. Aarunya was also worried after hearing the word attack and that too in the absence of her brother and father. She was worried not for realm or pupils; she was worried mostly for her gemstones. "I have predicted so many right things about you, just after your entry in my hut, if still, you doubt my words then you are the dumbest creature I have ever met," the old lady replied. Aarunya had no choice but to believe in her words.

"When should we start the process, I mean what I am required to do?" Aarunya asked. She had made up her mind to trust the words of the old lady and do what she asks her to do. The Old lady's prediction about the attack on her estate had freaked out Aarunya. The old lady asked them to come outside under the moonlight. They followed her orders.

While they were moving out, the old lady said, "Only the blood from Brahmins can perform this task." "No worry, my veins carry the blood of brahmin emperor," Aarunya replied with conceit. When Aarunya said so, Sahrindri smirked. It seemed like there was no such requirement of carrying the blood of brahmin to perform that task. Aarunya was too naïve to understand those conspires, she was lost in her obsession of becoming immortal and eternally beautiful. All that she understood was that Sahrindri cannot perform the task because she wasn't a brahmin.

The Old lady started collecting dry woods, perhaps she wanted to light a fire. Sahrindri helped her in the task. Aarunya was seeing them and was anxiously waiting for the rituals to be performed as soon as possible. She was looking at the sky, it was filled with stars, Aarunya couldn't identify which among them was the Sitara comet, she wasn't even sure if the Sitara comet was yet visible or not. She had just heard about sighting of Sitara comet that night. Her heart was pondering a lot of questions. Her heart was in a way worried about the attack, her estate might face and the other way it was excited too to gain powers from rituals of the old lady. Now she was dreaming herself to be the most powerful and beautiful lady of the planet, one who gained powers from today's rituals and the one who will soon wear the yellow gem as a ring in her hand.

Old lady lighted the fire on the woods. She asked Aarunya to sit down near the fire. It was a creepy scene. Nobody, not even animals were visible in the night and only three ladies sitting under the moonlight and near the fire. Old lady soon started chanting the mantras. She was mixing some sort of materials in the fire and was revolving around the fire and Aarunya. Sahrindri was watching all of it while standing quietly beside. For a reasonable time, she kept on chanting mantras and kept on revolving around the fire and Aarunya.

After chanting few more of mantras, the old lady went inside the hut and bought a bowl with her. Aarunya's eyes were all on her. The Old lady came near her. It was visible that there was blood in the bowl. "What is it?" Aarunya asked. "Human's blood," she replied in no time. She didn't hesitate to refer that blood as humans. There was certainly a sacrifice of human life in bringing that blood in that bowl. Still the old lady hasn't paused once to say those words in front of her.

Aarunya's eyes stretched in shock when she heard that it was human's blood. She didn't say anything, but her big beautiful eyes said a lot many things. Reading her eyes, the old lady whispered, "Every good thing requires sacrifices." Listening to her words, the lust of power, immortality, and beauty danced once more like a wave in the ocean of her heart. Aarunya smirked after hearing that.

Although she had a complete idea, what she needed to do with that blood, still for mere formality and confirmation, she asked her again, "And what I am supposed to do with it?" "Hold it first," said the old lady and handed bowl into Aarunya's hand, who was still sitting near the fire. "Drink it on the exact time, when I'll say, drink." Aarunya was quite sure that she is going to ask her to drink, still she didn't hesitate to perform the task. Old lady again started chanting mantras in front of the fire. She was still pouring some dark substance in the fire. Aarunya's eyes were revolving. Sometimes, her eyes were on fire, sometimes on the old lady and sometimes on the sky, in search of Sitara comet.

After five minutes of chanting, some disturbances happened in between the stars. Aarunya was still holding the bowl, and old lady was still chanting the mantras in front of the fire, when finally, the sitara comet arrived, old lady bawled, 'Drink.' Aarunya took no time in emptying the bowl down her throat. As soon she emptied the bowl, old lady cut Aarunya's arm from a knife. Blood started pouring from her hand.

"Aahh…!!!" She yelled in extreme pain. "Put it in fire," old lady instructed.

Aarunya was blindly following her instructions. She poured her drop of bloods in the fire. Old lady was still chanting the dark mantras. After a while, she stopped. Aarunya gave a look at her. Her arm was still bleeding. When the lady stopped chanting the mantras, Sahrindri came and tied her bleeding arm with a piece of cloth.

"Are we done now, am I eternally beautiful and young now?" asked Aarunya in enthusiasm. "Almost," said the old lady. "What else now?" she asked. "Now we are left with one last and one most important task," said the old lady. "And what is that?" Aarunya cried, her every word was saying that she was damn excited and impatient in completing the task. "You need to kill one of the people, you love," said the old lady.

Aarunya was still sitting near the fire. When she heard those words of old lady, she instantly got up from her place. Bowl of blood had fallen from her hand. "What…?" she yelled. Old lady had already performed all weird rituals. Right from her presence in the cemetery to her demand of asking Aarunya to drink human's blood, everything was creepy, and now she was asking her to kill someone she loves. "I can never kill someone I love," said Aarunya. Then the old lady started laughing loudly in her terrible voice. She was probably teasing Aarunya from her laughter. "That's the only choice to become powerful, immortal, eternally beautiful and…," while saying so, old lady stepped near Aarunya and continued, "And most importantly that's the only way to protect your gemstones," she emphasised about the protection of gemstones. She might know how important gemstones were for Aarunya.

"You need to kill someone you love," the old lady repeated. "You are mad!" said Aarunya. Old lady started laughing again in her petrifying voice. "I will never do that," said Aarunya with confidence in her voice. Old lady increased the volume of her laughter and said, "Soon, you'll do that... Soon."

Aarunya went near Sahrindri, held her hand and said, "Come on Sahrindri, we'll not stay here any longer." Sahrindri followed orders of her princess and moved with her. The old lady was still laughing in creepiest way. Aarunya and Sahrindri left her place.

They returned from the same dark forest, which was blessed by a cool breeze and full moonlight. "Sahrindri, why did you take me to this old creepy lady? She is mad and she can't do anything." Aarunya asked her on the way. "I am sorry Aarunya, I have heard about her from my sources," she replied. "Your all sources are lunatic and illogical. This lady seemed mad and she can do nothing that she was promising." Said Aarunya. "But she was aware of gemstones and the fact that your father and brother aren't at home. How is that possible?" Sahrindri raised valid doubts. "Now leave, we have to reach before morning."

Sahrindri and Aarunya made their way back home, before morning. Next morning, before Aarunya could wake up, Sahrindri got up and came out of the house. An ugly Brahmin with an open ponytail was waiting for her outside. She wanted to meet him without the knowledge of soldiers. She managed to do so. "Dark magic has entered inside her," said Sahrindri to the brahmin. "Agastya is happy from you," said the brahmin and handed a little bag full of golden coins to her. Sahrindri took them and went back to the house.

2

The Brahmin of Indragadh

After giving the golden coins to Sahrindri, Agastya moved towards his troop. Four soldiers were waiting for him to come. He went and sat on the chariot and ordered it to move. The chariot moved as per the directions. Agastya wanted to go back to his estate, he seemed a visitor in the estates of Krishnapur. After travelling for the whole day, he reached his destination, in the estate of King Ashoka. Ashoka was emperor of Indragadh, a realm with high honour, troops and wealth. Indragadh was situated just beyond the hills neighbouring the boundaries of Krishnapur. Between these two estates, there was one giant hill which separated them. There was a common river, 'Sarita,' whose water was shared by the two great realms.

From the red carpet, he entered the palace, where the King was waiting for him, sitting on his exquisite and demanding throne. "It must be really tiring and tedious to go Krishnapur and return back to Indragadh," asked The King sitting on the throne. "Fairly, it was," Agastya replied. Hall was full of ministers and soldiers of realm of Indragadh. Everyone except the king stood up to honour him. This implied that Agastya was given high honour by the king. Ashoka made gestures to him. He asked Agastya to sit right besides him. But instead climbing the stairs to grab the seat, he gave a pause.

"I need to have a word with you in isolation," said Agastya to the King sitting on the throne. Ashoka was bewildered to listen the unexpected demand of Agastya. Agastya had travelled overnight. King was expecting him to rest. Instead he not only visited the palace but demanded isolation too. He presumed that whatever the concern is, need immediate attention of king. He knew Agastya would not bother him for matters which did not require his attention. Thus, the king's concern about the matter heightened, as he could not foresee that what was of such urgence, that Agastya could not stop himself even for a minute.

The King left his throne and got up. On his one demand King got up, it was evident that Agastya received high honour and prestige from the King. The King got up and asked Agastya in gestures, to walk with him. From the main hall of the palace, they walked in a room where they could interact in peace.

"I am still wondering why you made a surprise visit to Krishnapur," Ashoka asked Agastya. Agastya took a deep breath, then he helped himself to get seated on the chair near the chair of the king. King Ashoka was still standing, that meant a lot. Agastya dared to sit before Ashoka. That denoted that Agastya was not just another minister of the realm, but someone who was close to the king, like his friend and more like his mentor. King Ashoka also took the weight off from his feet and sat down.

Agastya was still silent. He was so lost in thoughts, that he wasn't even answering to the king. "What is bothering the great Agastya, the beholder of unlimited knowledge and wisdom," said the king. "*There is nothing in the world that can bother an ugly brahmin,*" replied Agastya. His words made it clear that he wasn't at all ashamed of his ugly appearance and was proud of his traits of being a knowledgeable brahmin.

Ashoka smiled and asked, "Alright! Then may I know what the great ugly brahmin with knowledge and wisdom is thinking?" Now when Agastya referred himself, Ashoka agreed on the fact and asked him about his thoughts. "*Not all thoughts are meant to be delivered in the form of words,*" Agastya answered. He was an intellectual brahmin, and his words were proving that he was capable of playing with words, quite well. "Not even in front of me?" asked king Ashoka. This question of him was revealing the fact that he considered himself to be someone special to Agastya. "*When it comes to secret thoughts of an intellectual person, everyone is equal to anyone*," Agastya added those words without any facial expressions and without any sense of guilt on insulting the king on his face. "I cannot win with you in words," said Ashoka and surrendered himself in front of him. "*Those who opt to win with a sword can never win with words, but vice versa isn't true*," Agastya delivered another dialogue to counter the king in his own words. He was an eloquent orator. He played with words, better than one can play with swords or arches.

Thinking something, Ashoka said after a while, "When it comes to secret thoughts of an intellectual person, everyone is equal to anyone. Perhaps this is why you never shared with me, why being a brahmin your ponytail is open." When Ashoka said so, Agastya remained silent. Even Ashoka grieved to say so, he had asked Agastya many times about his open ponytail but Agastya never revealed the truth in front of him.

Ashoka changed the topic, "If you are done with your game of words, then can we proceed to discuss the matter for which you have asked for isolation," asked the king. "For sure, I have not even rested for a moment after coming from Krishnapur, just because I wanted to see you and talk to you," said Agastya to make him aware that he is more aggravated to talk about the matter.

"Spit it out," Ashoka ordered like a king. Agastya might have been a mentor or even a friend but a King is still a King, and everyone must adhere to the orders of the King. Agastya got up from his chair and walked to the window. Now instead of facing Ashoka, he was facing the window, where little Abhimanyu, prince of Indragadh was learning how to fight with a sword. Agastya's back was visible to Ashoka. Ashoka was still waiting for him to speak and reveal why he wanted to talk with him in such emergency and that too in isolation. "I think, within three-four days we should attack Krishnapur," Agastya followed his king's instructions and spit out the matter in just one line. His voice's tone didn't change a bit when he talked about attacking Krishnapur, the realm he had recently visited.

"What?" King Ashoka got up from his seat immediately after listening to his words. Ashoka knitted his brows, worry lines appeared on his forehead. He couldn't let go of the stress Agastya's statement caused him even after uttering, 'What' in shock. Agastya was still quietly looking at Abhimanyu, it seemed at the age of five, Abhimanyu was all prepared to lead a war. He didn't react to the word, 'What' and surprise of king Ashoka. "You have lost your senses," Ashoka said. Agastya still didn't react, he didn't even look back to see the curves of the forehead of Ashoka and to even react when Ashoka raised doubt on his senses.

"We share a friendly bond with the estate of Krishnapur. They are our neighbour. King Mahendra is like my friend," Ashoka presented his side of concern to Agastya. "*Friendship is a temporary relation, that changes in time and in accordance with need*," Agastya again played with his words. "But why you are even asking me to attack the realm of Krishnapur. What's the benefit? That estate is beyond the 'Sarita,' river and hill. Our people will never want to go beyond the hill," said Ashoka.

Ashoka had valid arguments. An attack on another estate isn't just similar to having another meal of the day. It is a sacrifice of hundreds of people from both sides. This sacrifice isn't just a piece of meal, which could be gulped down the throat, in just a few minutes of discussion. Agastya had not denoted any valid reason for the attack yet. He obviously needed to justify his great demand to the king. All of a sudden he had demanded an attack on an estate, therefore obviously he was expected to present valid grounds for the same. Although Ashoka has always blindly followed the instructions of Agastya but this time, it was something different which needed to be answered.

Agastya's eyes were still on little Abhimanyu, who was now taking some rest from the game of swords. "Right now we have only half access to Sarita river, but after winning the estate of Krishnapur, we'll not only have full access to Sarita river, but we'll also expand our territory," Agastya mentioned two reasons of attack in one breath. "We already have expanded territory. Moreover we are not short of water anyhow. There stands no valid reason of attack all of a sudden, especially to an estate with whom we share a friendly bond," Ashoka still denied the idea of attack on Krishnapur.

Agastya remained silent for another couple of seconds. Then while looking at Abhimanyu, he said, "our estate might not need expansion and our pupil might not need more water, but certainly little Abhimanyu needs a mother." Giving perplexed looks at Agastya, Ashoka asked, "What you mean?" Listening to this question, Agastya who was still looking at Abhimanyu from the window, turned towards Ashoka and said, "I have heard king Mahendra has one beautiful daughter named Aarunya who is just seventeen years' old," said Agastya, he hit arch on right spot, now he was waiting for Ashoka to react.

Ashoka felt numb for three seconds, he had heard a lot about the beauty of Aarunya. After thinking, Ashoka replied, "Why would I need to attack the realm of Krishnapur, I would simply go and ask for the hand of Aarunya to Mahendra, he would never deny me, he is my friend." "Oh! He will definitely deny you, why would he marry his pricelessly beautiful daughter to someone who is already married and has a son from his first wife," Agastya added some more points into the argument. "But I am a widower," said Ashoka to claim his eligibility to marry Aarunya. "That makes you none better for princess Aarunya, many kings are die heartedly waiting to marry her as their first and only wife" Agastya displayed the truth in front of the king.

Agastya could notice changes in facial expressions of Ashoka. The way he reacted at first on the matter of the attack on Krishnapur, it seemed that he would never adhere to the instructions of Agastya but soon after introducing Aarunya in the matter, his words of protest lessened and his tone changed. Now it seemed that a little more pressure from Agastya could turn Ashoka's no into a yes for instant war.

"But if I want to remarry, then certainly I have many other options, one who could fetch me a pretty wife without any war," said Ashoka. Agastya smiled, took a second's pause and replied, "Nature has bestowed unparalleled beauty to Aarunya." After saying so, Agastya again turned towards the window, where Abhimanyu again started playing with swords. With his age, he seemed intellectual, and it could be predicted that in the near future he'll be a great swordsman.

Agastya was waiting for Ashoka to reply on Aarunya's beauty's appraisals. "Even if I agree for an attack, why are you insisting on doing it in next two three days.,. Our soldiers aren't really prepared for a war," Ashoka made his point with clarity. He was right on his stand that all of a sudden troops and army of the realm cannot be prepared for a war and that too on a nation which is capable of fighting back with same forces and power.

Agastya again turned and shifted his eyes from Abhimanyu to his father. "Do you really think that troops need to be prepared. What if someone attacks on your realm, right now? What you are going to do? Obviously, soldiers are prepared for the war 24*7. This is just an excuse to avoid the war, I believe coming Saturday is perfect for an attack as per astrological conditions, we'll win the war if we'll attack coming Saturday" Agastya attacked Ashoka with words. Being a brahmin, he mentioned some astrological features too when to attack. "You are not talking about an attack on an ordinary kingdom. Krishnapur is not only blessed with good arm force, but king Mahendra has great leadership qualities, he cannot be defeated easily. Moreover, my son is five-year-old, I don't have anyone's support in the war, but his son…., his son is an equal hand for him in the war," Ashoka argued.

Agastya was demanding war with a powerful estate, whose king and prince were well-known fighters. Ashoka being a king could not say an instant yes in greed of a beautiful princess. He needed to be convinced that if he leads a war, the sacrifice of his soldiers will not go waste and he should definitely come back to his realm with the princess.

Agastya was smiling on Ashoka's argument. "May I know the reason behind that evil smile," said Ashoka reading the mind of Agastya. "King Mahendra and his son Aarav are not present in their estate, they have gone Ratnagadh. Indragadh would easily attain victory over Krishnapur with flying colours," Agastya replied. "So this was the reason of your sudden visit to Krishnapur," Ashoka inferred. "*Like words, not every action is meant to be told to everyone.*" I had so many purposes of visiting Krishnapur, but among them, this one was productive for you, that's why I shared with you," Agastya added to create more of bafflement in Ashoka's mind.

"But how coward we will be if we attack in the absence of king and prince," said Ashoka after a while. Being a ruler of an eminent empire, it would definitely not suit him to attack another empire when the king and prince of that empire aren't present in the estate. Agastya was plausibly waiting for such words from Ashoka, he was all prepared with words in his mind to counter this. "That won't be being a coward, that would be an intelligent sign of an emperor who intellectually expands his territory," said Agastya.

Agastya wanted an attack on coming Saturday at any cost. He was trying by all his intelligence to make Ashoka say yes. Ashoka started walking in the room. He probably thought what to do and what not to. Agastya gave him enough time to think and speak. Ashoka was still baffled to utter anything. When he took more than half a minute to reply, Agastya again shifted his eyes to Abhimanyu. "Enough for today, I am tired now. Need some rest," said Abhimanyu to his tutor. Agastya smiled at his imperial behaviour. He could see a coming emperor in him.

"No matter how good servants are; every child needs a mother for his better upbringing. After all a human need not to become just a swordsman, he needs to be a better human too," said Agastya to make Ashoka realise the needs of Abhimanyu. Ashoka still didn't say anything. Agastya keenly wanted to hear a yes from him, but he was an intellectual person with patience. He could never utter even a single wrong word, which could make Ashoka say a no for final. He was craftily displaying his words in front of him.

After a short halt Agastya said, "*No matter how beautiful whores are, they could never replace a wife.*" Now he had hit the perfect arch. This arch went straight on the goal. Agastya knew that king Ashoka wasn't just lusty but was a seeker of true love in his wife. when this love can be given by a beautiful and young lady, why wouldn't he give a chance.

"I am still afraid of saying a yes for a war," said Ashoka. "I am sure the word afraid is mistakenly used in your words. Else the great king Ashoka wouldn't be fearful of anyone, especially not from a realm which is free of his king and prince. A troop which is not led by a good leader can never win a war, no matter how good the soldiers are," said Agastya to confirm why the great king Ashoka used the word fear for a war.

Ashoka closed his eyes, his eyebrows twisted a bit. It seemed Agastya misunderstood his statement and Ashoka was bewildered to see how a person like Agastya who could play with words, is misunderstanding his words. "How did your wisdom allowed you to interpret my words as fear of a war?" said Ashoka. "Then what do you mean?" Agastya surrendered immediately. That was also a sign of an intellectual personality, one who is not afraid of accepting his fault and one who is always ready to learn something new.

Ashoka went near the chair and took off weight from his feet. He placed his elbow on his knee and hand on his face. His body language was depicting that he was still wondering what is right and what is wrong. Agastya was happy to notice that at least he was giving a thought to say yes. "If not fear of losing the war, then what is bothering you," Agastya again asked him the reason of his worry.

Ashoka moved his hand from his face and placed on his thigh. He then tilted his chin and raised his face to answer Agastya. "I am afraid of being called a coward to attack a realm when the king and prince are absent," said Ashoka. Being the emperor of a great empire, his fear was all justified. Now Agastya had to play his best cards, to make him say yes. Agastya moved towards his chair and sat down. Now physically he was very close to king Ashoka. He placed his hand on his thigh and said, "Were you aware of the fact that king Mahendra and prince Aarav aren't present in their realm." Looking in his eyes,

Ashoka realised what Agastya meant to say. Agastya didn't miss any opportunity to win Ashoka over.

"You are more cunning than my mere imagination," said Ashoka and smirked. This smirk of him said a lot to Agastya. He was happy in his heart after an affirmative reaction from Ashoka's side. He was elated by gaining that silent consent from Ashoka, but a clever person always hides his extremes, whether in happiness or in sadness. In his heart, he was dancing in joy, but by face he didn't even smile to make anyone see that he was on the seventh cloud by gaining that silent consent from Ashoka.

"I am just wondering why and how this war will benefit you," said Ashoka. His concern was valid as the way Agastya wanted the war to happen, it seemed that the war will provide personal leverage to him. "Whatever I am doing is in the interest of realm," said Agastya. "And I trust you on that. Your father served my father, we share relations from our ancestors," Ashoka uttered words to prove his never changing trust on Agastya's every word.

Though Ashoka had not said yes with words but his reaction had made it obvious. To confirm his yes, Ashoka said, "I think we must discuss the matter with other ministers as well," said Ashoka. "Well I think otherwise...," Agastya again made a doubtful clause. Ashoka didn't say anything, he was waiting for Agastya to clarify on his own. Agastya added, "I am thinking to inform ministers about the matter." He replaced the word, 'discuss' with the word, 'inform.' Clearly, Ashoka or any other person could never win from him in words. Ashoka smiled on his deviousness in words.

Soon Ashoka called a meeting of every important minister of his kingdom. In an hour, everyone gathered in the room. Everyone was seated on their positions, and the meeting was headed by king Ashoka. Agastya was also present in the meeting. He took his chair like any other ordinary meeting of the realm. In public Ashoka and Agastya never demonstrated their personal relations but everyone knew that they were very close to each other and king could never deny any proposal of Agastya.

Everyone took around a minute to settle down at their positions in their meetings. "What was so urgent that you called an emergency meeting?" said one of the ministers. King Ashoka who was sitting on the throne, got up.

"I thank you all for coming on such short notice," said king Ashoka to start with a formal greeting. "We are planning an attack on Krishnapur in next three-four days," in one breathe and in another dialogue, he delivered the purpose of calling the meeting on such short notice. Soon after he delivered the purpose, colour of every face present there changed. Every eye stretched in wonder, and every lip soon started gossiping to each other about the matter.

While everyone was busy talking with themselves, the chief of soldiers said, "Why did you take such a decision all of sudden." When he was speaking, he was looking towards Agastya. He plausibly had all idea, who was behind this shocking decision. When Agastya found him looking at him, he shifted his eyes to king Ashoka and said, "Your Highness! You need to answer us all, why such crucial decision all of sudden?" He played his another card impulsively. As he found that other ministers might guess that he is behind the war. And if they do that they might deny the proposal. The reason behind their probable denial was hidden enviousness towards Agastya by all.

Ashoka tried his best not to smile after hearing Agastya's statement. One more time he admired Agastya's cunning intelligence. Then Ashoka waited for everyone to settle down their gossips. After a while when everyone was silent, he said, "for a long time I had been thinking that our people need full access to Sarita river and by gaining control over Krishnapur, we will not only gain access of Sarita river, but our territory will expand beyond the hill from where Sarita river emerges." He demonstrated a few points to justify his attack on Krishnapur. Agastya's company have made him learn, how to handle people with words. Deceitfully he did hide that his chief purpose of the attack was princess Aarunya.

"There is no shortage of water in our estate, then why to sacrifice lives of soldiers just to expand the territory," said one of the ministers. Another minister added, "My lord! Sorry to disagree but how can we plan an attack on an estate with whom we share a friendly bond of years." King Ashoka was probably expecting such questions from his ministers, that's why he was all prepared. "There is no permanent friend nor permanent enemy in politics. It will be a great opportunity for us to expand our territory, beyond the hill," said king Ashoka to satisfy the ministers.

But it wasn't an easy task to satisfy the ministers about an immediate attack on an estate. One of the ministers said, "Your Highness! Are you even aware that you are talking about an attack on a brahmin estate? Brahmin emperor will win over us mostly by their mental power." Now king Ashoka wanted to hide the fact that the emperor and his son is not present in the palace. "I am a true Rajput emperor, I would call myself the most coward emperor if I get petrified by any emperor because of his caste or his intelligence," said king Ashoka. He played smartly with him. The minister didn't dare to protest again.

Soon after he was done, chief of soldiers asked, "But why this attack all of a sudden, our soldiers aren't even prepared." Agastya who was silent till now, opened his mouth to say,

"Here I am with the king. Every soldier is prepared to fight for his realm every time." King Ashoka repeated Agastya's words, which he had said to him in personal. "What if any another kingdom attacks us today, will we ask them for preparation or will we fight them back," said Ashoka.

For once no one dared to speak when Ashoka delivered such heavy words. After a while chief of soldiers said, "You are the king, we'll have to follow your orders. I'll go and train our soldiers to get ready for the attack." "I am glad you are co-operating," said king Ashoka and the meeting was terminated. When everyone left, Agastya stayed back to exchange a few more words with Ashoka in solitude. "I am glad you didn't tell them that king Mahendra and prince Aarav are not present in their realm. I was afraid you would spit out the truth," said Agastya. "Well, I have spent three years of my life with you. I can't be that naïve."

3

Ancestors

King Mahendra, father of Aarunya was about to reach Ratnagadh with his son Aarav. The estate of Ratnagadh was located in deserts and was around two days away from Krishnapur. Mahendra was travelling with enough soldiers who could protect them and serve them in the way. The troop rested, as water was needed to quench the thirst of horses. "Although we have almost reached but still I want some rest, place the tent here," said king Mahendra to his soldiers. He was travelling for the entire day, so it was quite obvious that he and his son would be tired of travelling. Even the horses needed some rest.

Soldiers started placing the tent for the rest of the troop. Mahendra while waiting for the tent to be placed, set himself at a little distance from other soldiers. Aarav followed him in his solitude. "Father," he said softly. Mahendra looked at him, waiting for him to utter some more of words. "When you are planning to tell me that how you are going to awaken those sleeping gemstones?" Aarav asked. Looking in his eyes, Mahendra replied, "Soon." So it seemed that he was still not in the mood to tell his son what was the matter.

"I don't understand that when Aarunya can know everything then why can't I?" Aarav asked in an irritating voice. "I was not the person who shared everything with Aarunya. It was your grandmother," king Mahendra replied. "Unlike me, Aarunya was crafty enough to extract the truth from her," Aarav mentioned that it was his sister who was cunning to learn the truth from their dead grandmother. "She wasn't crafty, she loved your grandmother, and she spent most of her time with her, unlike you," king Mahendra defended his daughter.

"Whatever, we have almost reached there, are you in any mood to tell me now. Aarunya is younger than me. Still she knows everything about gemstones. Isn't this unfair with me?" Aarav demanded to learn everything about gemstones once more. "I am already regretting that Aarunya learned the truth from my mother at the wrong time. She is now obsessed with the power of gemstones. She doesn't know the fact that awakening gemstones will be a great sacrifice. Your grandmother told her more about gemstones and its powers and less about ancestors," said Mahendra.

With his words, he was clear that he wasn't lusty of the power of gemstones. "I am hearing this since my birth that ancestors need to be saved, but no one had ever told me in what danger ancestors are in and if they are ancestors then how they are alive, why and how they need to be saved. What's the relation of it to gemstones and….," he kept on asking endless questions? "Give a break to your questions," said king Mahendra in between. "But I am not asking these questions at a wrong time. Soon we'll be in the palace of Ratnagadh. I am sure the palace of Ratnagadh is not the right place to talk about the matter. Then why not now and here?" said Aarav.

Before Mahendra could answer him anything, one of their soldiers came and said, "My lord! The tent is ready; you can have some rest." So the soldiers were done with their job of getting the king and prince comfortable for some time. The full day's journey was obviously tiring. King Mahendra and prince Aarav went inside the tent. After getting seated comfortably, king asked soldiers to leave them in peace. Aarav was glad to find that his father was in the mood to share some secrets about gemstones with him.

"So I believe now you are in the mood to talk with me about gemstones," said Aarav. Mahendra smiled and replied, "Yes.

I'll answer some of your questions." So he was only prepared to answer some questions and was in the mood to still hide some. The more he denied to share the secret, the more Aarav was craving to know of it. "Still some," said Aarav to let him know that he does not like the fact that king Mahendra is still in the mood to share incomplete information with him. "You should be glad that at least I am sharing some answers," said Mahendra.

Aarav had no other option, except to listen to whatever information was being provided to him. King Mahendra didn't say anything, he was waiting for Aarav to again put up questions. "How are gemstones so powerful that Aarunya is so obsessed with them?" Aarav asked his first question. King Mahendra was now expected to deliver him his answers. He was sitting on quite a distance from Mahendra. He stood up and came near to Aarav.

In very less audible voice, he said, "the one who will wear the awakened gemstones in their hand as the ring will be immortal and eternally young and beautiful." "What!" the word came out of Aarav's mouth as if he felt the most surprising shock of his entire life. "I don't believe this," he added. "It is true my son," king Mahendra assured him that whatever he was saying was all true. Aarav's eyes were saying that he was still in shock and could not believe what he had just heard. "Not only this, the holder of gem will be one of the most powerful creatures on the planet, no one else can beat awakened gem holders in war," king Mahendra added.

King Mahendra had said something that Aarav couldn't bring himself to believe easily. Promise of immortality, young and beautiful body and non-beatable life, these all abilities of mere four colourful stones couldn't be gulped by Aarav easily. "But then what about ancestors," asked Aarav. He was quite right in asking that. Every time the king referred to the purpose of awakening gemstones it was always saving the ancestors. King Mahendra went silent after listening to that. "That's a long story," he replied. "I want to hear that now," Aarav demanded. "Even I don't know that, completely," said king Mahendra. Aarav gave perplexed looks, as his father was working on something since years and still he was saying the words, 'I don't know completely.' After having devoted a major part of his life to awakening of gemstones, Aarav was expecting that his father knew everything.

King Mahendra was in the mood of telling everything he knew about gemstones to Aarav. Aarav could predict this as he was answering all his questions. "Tell me whatever you know," said Aarav. Aarav asked a smart question, in which he demanded to ask whatever his father knew about gemstones and ancestors. Now king Mahendra was expected to deliver honest answers to him. "All that I know is told to me by my father," king Mahendra mentioned. "And my grandfather must have known this fact by his father and the cycle goes on," asked Aarav. "Yes," replied the king.

Aarav was asking so because Mahendra had mentioned that ancestors needed to be saved and ancestors must be forefathers of Aarav who needs to be saved with the help of gemstones It means that since generations, their family was trying to save their ancestors but failing and consequently those people are referred to as ancestors. "What did your father tell you," asked Aarav, requesting his father to continue.

After a suitable pause king Mahendra started speaking. "Father told me that there are four souls trapped in four gemstones since many years and as and when the gemstones would be awakened, those souls would be released and freed from irresistible pain and agony of years. One of those souls belong to our family; that soul is our ancestor. We share blood with that soul, it is our duty to save that soul from the pain. Even the other three gemstones have captured the soul of someone's ancestors. This is why our family has been saying since years that ancestors need to be saved." King Mahendra spit out whatever he knew in one breathe.

"Who trapped them in gemstones and how, and how that coronet is in our family for so long?" Aarav asked as per his anxiety. Those questions might sprout in anyone's head who might listen about gemstones from king Mahendra. "I don't know the answer of any such question, who, why and how trapped ancestors in those gemstones. I just know that four souls are trapped in gemstones since years and we need to save them, we need to end their pain," said king Mahendra.

Aarav was listening about gemstones with all his interest. His questions were being answered after years. He had waited for a long time to listen to the answers, he deserved to listen. After a while, he further asked, "But how do gemstones promise endless powers, immortality and beauty of eternity. How are you so sure about that? These two things have nothing to do with each other." That was a sensible question. Four souls were trapped in four gemstones, that was one thing and those gemstones can provide endless power, immortality and eternal beauty to the one holding them was another thing. However, those two different things weren't contradictory but also had nothing common with each other.

King Mahendra sighed on this question and answered, "Now that's another different story." "I hope this one you know completely," said Aarav. His account was coherent as last time when king Mahendra talked about a long story, he couldn't narrate it completely to Aarav. This time Aarav was hoping to listen to the complete story from his father. "I also hope so," king Mahendra replied in rather a cynical way. He wasn't sure, whether he knew the complete truth about powers of gemstones or not, there was no way he could tell the complete truth to Aarav.

Aarav was happy that at least his father was telling him whatever he knew. However, he couldn't figure it out why his father made him wait so long. "Well, then tell me whatever you know. Tell me how you are so sure about such powers of gemstones?" Aarav repeated his question. King Mahendra and Aarav was sitting on two small wooden stools, placed by their soldiers for their comfort. Even in tent, king and prince couldn't rest on the floor, those were the privileges of being king and prince. Soldiers need to carry all the things that might be needed on the way for royal people's comfort and luxury.

He stood up from his stool and moved two-three steps ahead. Aarav was still sitting on his position and was waiting for him to answer his question. "This coronet is in our family since many generations, and since generations, kings are trying to save ancestors. Sometimes they try through some sacred mantras, sometimes through black magic, etc. In short, they are giving all their efforts, to end the pain of ancestors, but all are failing in their efforts. Last time it was tried by my father." King Mahendra gave a pause after saying so.

Aarav who was still sitting got up. His father was facing his back towards him. Aarav went near him and asked, "How did grandfather tried to save them?" when Aarav asked this question, king Mahendra closed his eyes, his facial expressions said that it wasn't something pleasant. "That's how he died," King replied. Though his eyes didn't tear when he said so, but his face was speaking out his grief. Aarav kept quiet, he wanted his father to himself to continue. He started narrating the story to Aarav.

4

Agastya's Chamber

Agastya returned home with a smile on his face. He was elated in his heart because everything was happening the way he wanted. When he entered home, he found his mother was waiting for him for dinner. "Mother I have asked you a hundred times, to eat food on time and not to wait for me," he said to his mother. "I am not in the habit of eating alone. After your father passed away, you are the only one I have., Why will I not wait for you?" said his mother. Agastya didn't say anything and went to wash his hands. After cleaning his hands, he came and sat on the floor to get done with dinner.

While serving him, his mother said, "At such an old age, you are making me prepare dinner for you." "I have asked you so many times, if you want help, then I can provide you from the palace. King Ashoka would send tens of servants for us in a second. But it's you who doesn't want help," Agastya retorted to his mother. "You can enjoy food either of your mother's hand or your wife's. No servant can replace that," his mother argued. "What about the kings then?" Agastya asked. "They are in the habit of eating food from servants." "You just stop arguing and tell me when you are planning to get married," asked his mother in irritation. "I have been waiting for a daughter in law for so long.," she added.

Taking a short pause Agastya asked, "Mother you have adopted me before three years as your child or as a source of daughter in law in near future." "Ssshhh! Keep quite. No one except you, your father and me are aware of the fact that you are not a brahmin, you are adopted by us before three years. Better not to repeat these words, else no one in the realm will respect you the way they do right now," said his mother. "Then better don't ask me for marriage, ever again," Agastya proclaimed in a rather harsh tone. His mother thought it's better not to talk about the matter.

It was really strange to see why an old lady would adopt an adult, especially just three years ago. Why she had adopted him in her grey hair. Who adopts a child in their old age? People in those days usually did such things when they were young, if their wife was unable to conceive a child of their own. Further, it was also hard to figure out why an adult like Agastya had thrown himself under the supervision of an old couple. For a second, one could believe that Agastya might have done so because he was looking to pretend his identity to be that of a brahmin so that he could rule over Ashoka and Indragadh. But why his guardian parents did so was still difficult to understand.

The way Agastya reacted on the topic of marriage was something that could not be digested easily. Any parent, whether biological or guardian, wishes to see their child get married at the right age. Agastya's guardians were none different. But, certainly, Agastya was different in this context. It was time to go to bed. Before sleeping, Agastya went to check on his mother. He found her sleeping peacefully. Then he came back to his room and locked the door. Then he went to a shelf and drew a dagger from the shelf. He ran the dagger across his left wrist without blinking and collected the dripping blood in a bowl. He then poured some herbs on the wound so that the blood would stop coming out.

He then opened his entire cupboard and placed all the items out of the cupboard. From his cupboard, an entire secret chamber opened. Staircases were going down. Agastya stepped down. The room was horrible. It was full of dark magic items. Human scalps, bones, and other dark magic items were loaded into the room. He then gave a look at the room. There were four subdivisions of the room. Every division has one gate. One gate had a big picture of a yellow gem; one had a blue gem; one had a green gem; and the last one had a red gem.

Agastya carried the bowl inside the chamber, which had his blood in it. After entering the chamber, he divided the blood into four different bowls and then headed towards the gate that had the yellow gem's picture on it. When he entered the inside, the scenario of the room was horrible. One could miss his heartbeat after having just one glimpse.

A man was chained to the walls and he was bleeding from every pore of his body. He was totally desiccated. Flesh from his body was drained out like water from a dry river. It looked like his hair, beard, and moustaches had not been shaved for centuries. Two pieces of clothing on his body were torn and could barely cover his body. When Agastya entered, he gave him a look. Seeing him, the man in the miserable condition smirked and said, "You're back again!"

Anyone who might give a look at him would cry their hearts out at his pathetic condition. One's soul would come out seeing his wounds and blood. Still, in that pale and pathetic condition, he dared to smirk and utter those audacious words. Agastya didn't react, as if he was very sure that the chained man would react similarly.

"A century passed, but nothing could take away your arrogance, your hate, your abhorrence, your..." Agastya tried to speak, but before he could finish, the desiccated man interrupted, "Just pour your blood down my throat and leave me alone." Agastya cracked his wicked laughter at his words and said, "So you yourself are asking to pour my blood down your throat. Does this mean that you yourself wish to live more and rot like an insect in the pits of hell for eternity?" " Does my wish matter? Won't you anyway want me to rot in the pits of hell for eternity? "

Agastya didn't even take a second's pause. "Exactly," he said, and poured the bowl's blood down his throat. Then he locked the room and headed towards the room that had the door with Blue Gem's picture. Another desiccated human was chained behind the door of this chamber as well. The only difference here was that there was a female behind this door. When Agastya entered, the woman in chains didn't react at all. Her ignorance probably hurt his ego. "So how are you celebrating the century of misery and pain?" "Let me out of the chain and then I'll show you..." The lady went beyond control. She cried in pain and yelled like a beast. Her painful voice solved Agastya's purpose. He smirked and sighed like a devil. Agastya said, "I can hear you yelling in pain for an eternity," said Agastya, and again poured his blood down her throat.

Then he headed towards the door that had Green Gem's picture on it. Another dessicated human, this time a man. Agastya didn't bother to react or exchange words with this one. He just poured his blood down his throat and came out. Even the man inside didn't react. The hate of Agastya towards this man was a little less than others.

Then he moved towards the last gate, the one that had a red-colured gem's picture over it. This time, behind the walls, there was no dessicated human. Instead, there was a young and very attractive lady dressed in red. "Hello, Bitch!" said Agastya. While looking at him, she smirked and said, "Could you please stop calling me a bitch?" Don't you know that the community of dogs is known to be loyal? " "Agreed! I will invent another word for you. The most abusive word for the lady who betrayed her... Agastya tried to say something, but the lady wouldn't let him. "Shut up and end your rant, just give me the damn bowl." She said and snatched the bowl and drank his blood. She then stepped outside the gate. "See you after a fortnight, when I will again need your blood for survival." She said and went out of the chamber and then out of his home. Agastya didn't stop her.

5

Tries of king Dharmendra

Twenty-five years ago, in the palace of Krishnapur.

King Dharmendra, father of King Mahendra and his mother Sumitra, were talking in their room. No one was allowed to enter and disturb them in their solitude. "I have tried every possible thing in my life to save ancestors, but I failed terribly," said king Dharmendra to his wife. "Don't call yourself a failure. You should be proud of yourself that you tried every possible thing and I have seen you sacrificing all your life in quest of saving ancestors," said the queen to console her husband.

Royal generations of estate Krishnapur were trying to save their ancestors but yet no-one had ever been successful in doing so. King Dharmendra was no different. "Like my father I don't want to pass this burden on my son Mahendra, he is not even married yet. I know the agony of seeing this bloody coronet every time and imagining my own ancestors are suffering in this, I don't wanna let Mahendra know about the same," said king Dharmendra in grief. It was obvious that every king who came to know about the gemstones worried that their ancestor's souls are suffering in gemstones. The agony of not being able to do anything for them is miserable, king Dharmendra knew this pain, and that is why he wanted to not to pass on this pain to his son.

"You are true, Mahendra is not even married yet, he won't be able to take the burden of saving the ancestors," said the queen after a while. "Only the one who had made these gemstones sleep can tell us how to awaken these gemstones," Queen added. She perhaps meant that her husband was irrational to look after something which is impossible and he must now stop trying. When she thought that she can't say him so in gestures, she used words to say so, "You must stop looking after the measure to awaken these gemstones and stop this legacy right here. Don't pass it on to Mahendra."

King looked at her fiercely and said, "how can you be so selfish in saying so Sumitra?" "I am not selfish; I am rather practical. Now, what's the proof that really there is one soul trapped in one of these gemstones of your ancestors. You don't even know since how many generations, this coronet has been passed on to you all," said queen to stick on her point of leaving the gemstones matter. "You are asking of proof; this is legacy of our family. Can't you see these aren't ordinary stones? I haven't seen this size of gemstones anywhere in the world, except in our palace," king defended his point.

He was right in his context; those gemstones weren't ordinary looking gemstones. Just by looking at them anyone could tell that those gemstones aren't ordinary gem but are magical and might contain supernatural powers. But the queen was seeing his husband suffering in his life with anxiety of gemstones. She had seen him burning in rage of regret of not been able to do something to awaken those gemstones and release the soul of their ancestor. She had seen him passing his whole life in the dedication of one goal of awakening the gemstones and releasing the souls of ancestors. She obviously did not want the same fate for her child, Mahendra.

When king Dharmendra referred that he has not seen this big gemstones in his life except in his palace, he got an idea. "It might be possible that our palace is hiding some secrets about gemstones," said the king. "What you mean?" queen reacted.

"I mean our palace is so big, even I haven't seen every possible corner in my entire life. This coronet is in our palace since generations, there must be something hidden in this palace only which might reveal something about gemstones," said the king. King added, "Ever since Mahendra noticed Agastya had teared some pages, I am quite sure that there is something hidden in our palace as well." "But how we are going to identify what might relate to gem or ancestors,"the queen asked. "I don't know." They were just guessing that they might find something in palace which might relate to the gemstones but none of them were sure what that thing might be and how that should relate to gemstones and coronet.

"Even if we'll ask servants to look into the palace then what we'll have to tell them about gemstones," the queen asked a valid question again. The coronet and gemstones were passed on to the generations of the royal family of Krishnapur, but no one else except the royal persons was aware of the gemstones or coronet. "This is why we won't ask servants to look into the palace. We will do it by our self," King proclaimed in confidence. Queen didn't say anything in response. She was frustrated by her husband's madness of saving the ancestors.

Then soon after when King got the idea of looking into the palace. King and queen started looking for something valuable which might relate to gemstones and coronet. When Mahendra found them in hunt of the palace, he several times asked them but every time king and queen denied him to say anything. Every time when servants asked for help, they too were denied.

Looking into the entire palace wasn't an easy task. King and queen looked for days in their own palace but didn't find anything. "It's been three days since we started looking for something in the palace. But we didn't find anything that might relate. For how many more days are you going to do this?" the queen asked in frustration. "I won't give up easily. If I have got this idea, then this is definitely god's sign to help me. Palace's left section's basement is still something we haven't searched. That's my last hope. Who knows we might find something there," said the king with hope. "But that side is least visited by anyone in our family. Who will put anything valuable there?" queen asked. "It's the least visited that's what makes it more vulnerable to find anything there," king replied.

Then soon king and queen started looking in palace's left section's basement. For hours they searched keenly but didn't find anything. When they were about to give up, queen Sumitra said, "What's this?" she referred to five thick books lying in a safe. Four books carried four gemstones pictures, and one book carried the coronet's picture. The coronet wasn't carrying gemstones in the picture. "It's everything that we need, "the king said. His eyes were glittering in joy, he found everything that he needed. Finally, he was one step closure to awaken those beautiful sleeping gemstones.

They took the books with them in their room. "You should be thanking me, I found them first," queen didn't forget to take credits. "I owe you that," king gave her credits with due respect. Now when they were about to open books, king's hands shivered. "Why this fear now?" queen asked. "This is because I am on the edge of discovering the truth about gemstones, I am worrying what would happen if I fail even after knowing.," said the king. "Hope for the best and open the books," queen consoled him.

With shivering hands, he opened them, and he was right in his fear. Those books were written in a foreign language. "What kind of language is this?" said the king. Then the queen too noticed that those were written in some foreign language. Their joy and elation vanished in just one second. Just few minutes before they were on cloud nine that they found something which might help them in awakening those gemstones and now in just another minute, those five thick books were just bunch of papers for them. King's face's colour changed in just a few seconds. He was totally disappointed. After a while, he asked, "Where did you find these books?" he asked. "In a box which was hidden behind one painting," the queen replied. "Were there more books or something else there?" king asked in excitement and hope. "I don't remember exactly, but yes there was one more book, but I didn't pay attention to that, as these five covered everything, all gemstones, and the coronet, "the queen replied. "No we didn't find book on the transparent gem behind the coronet and there might be a translation," said King. One more time hope's ray covered in both of their eyes. With light's speed, they both went back to the basement and bought that book with them. One more time the king was in the hope that he might unlock everything about gemstones and the process of awakening them.

Hastily they went again in the basement and bought the remaining book with them. This time they were happy that this book wasn't written in a foreign language. This book was written in Sanskrit language, one which king and queen could understand. They started reading the book. The book started saying about the power of gemstones. It defined how different colours gemstones got power. Yellow from the sun, blue from water, red from human's blood and green from plants. Book didn't mention the transparent gemstone behind the coronet. That book said that the holder of gemstones will get immortality, eternal beauty and endless power to conquest the world.

King Dharmendra and queen Sumitra wanted to find out whether the book contains the secret of how to awaken the gemstones. But that book was very thin, in comparison to other four books of gemstones and coronet. Mostly it said about powers of gemstones. Then reading further king and queen reached to its section where it mentioned about how to awaken gemstones.

But again this time too they were disappointed as the further pages of books were torn and destroyed. Only one page was available regarding awakening the gemstones. That one page asked king Dharmendra to perform some rituals in the night when Sitara comet will appear in the sky. It talked about dark magic and drinking humans blood in the cemetery.

"I will perform the said rituals and will think what to do further," said king Dharmendra. "Are you out of your mind? This is all dark magic, and it might harm you. I will never allow you to put your life on risk," said queen Sumitra in anger. "I am left with no option, further it's mention here that doing this dark magic on sitara night might reduce the effect" King argued. "But it is not even the full method. What will you do after it?" the queen asked. "At least I'll be one step closer to save the ancestors. I'll do whatever it takes," king was determined that he is gonna perform the rituals.

Even after numerous denials of the queen, king secretly called one lady who could perform dark magic. King was lucky that soon the night arrived when Sitara comet was expected to appear in the sky. "I am leaving for something important. Something for which I have waited all my life. Something for which my family's generations have been waiting. Pray for my success, queen," said king Dharmendra to the queen. "More than anything I am gonna pray for your wellbeing," the queen replied. Her tone was saying that she was petrified of the dark magic king was gonna perform, and its dark consequences.

King changed his attire and wore the clothes of a normal common man. He took the book with him and went towards the cemetery in the midnight. There one old lady was waiting for him. King Dharmendra handed the book to her. King was crafty enough to show her only the pages of awakening gemstones. He deviously hid the title and asked her to perform the written rituals. He wanted to keep the secret of gemstones from everyone except his royal family.

After reading the mantras, the old lady said, "I have spent most of my life in performing dark magic, still have never heard such dark mantras." King didn't react at it, he wanted the task to be done as soon as possible. She added, "I am afraid, the consequences of these mantras could be scarier than your imagination." "I am up for anything," King asserted that he had made mind to give whatever it takes.

Old lady lighted the fire and prepared other stuff. Soon she started chanting the dark mantras and started revolving around the fire and the king. She took reasonable time of reciting mantras. She then gave him the bowl full of human's blood. Then she again started chanting the mantras. Then soon when the Sitara comet arrived, she asked the king to drink the same. King gulped down the blood in no time. The old lady performed all other rituals. Then she did cut his hand and poured blood from his blood in the fire. After that, she chanted some more mantras.

King Dharmendra was all the time wondering about saving the ancestors. Not even for a second, he gave a thought about the powers, he might attain from the dark magic. "It's done," she said. The king got up, handed her a bag of golden coins. "I repeat I am not responsible for any of the consequences of this dark magic," she said. "Don't worry, I am prepared for everything," said the king and left.

But the consequences of that dark magic were worse than mere imaginations. Soon after the dark magic entered inside, the king felt various changes in him. Whenever he saw the queen, he felt like some force is asking him to kill her. He could not perceive what was happening within him, but the dark magic was asking him to gain power by killing someone he loved. He didn't know from where those urges were coming in him, but all that he wanted was to kill the queen. He felt like he'll become powerful if he kills the queen.

For days he tried to stop himself from doing so. But day by day those urges kept increasing. At last, he made a suicide note for his son, Mahendra. In his suicide note, he mentioned everything about gemstones and ancestors. He had written in words, the pain and agony he had bear all his life for not been able to save his ancestors. He too wanted to pass on this legacy of responsibility of trying to save the ancestors to his soon. He mentioned about books too and his practice of dark magic which was forcing him to kill someone he loved. He felt that he could do anything to save ancestors but cannot kill his own wife. That's the reason he was taking that bold step of committing suicide. After handing over the suicide note and coronet to Mahendra, king Dharmendra committed suicide.

King Mahendra was done reciting the entire story to his son prince Aarav. After he was done, he looked back at prince Aarav. He was expressionless. "Father…," prince Aarav said those words in a heavy tone. "Yes." "I am glad that unlike grandfather, you choose to share the burden of saving the ancestors with me," Aarav expressed his gratitude. "Our generations have been trying to awaken these gemstones but failing. I did not choose it on my own. I knew it would take more, I knew your help is requisite in this," king Mahendra admitted.

"But then, why are you upset that grandmother shared everything with Aarunya," Aarav asked after a while. The king who was looking into eyes of Aarav, moved his chin down, his eyes too started looking downwards. He folded his hand and turned around. It seemed he wasn't about to tell something that would be easy to tell and listen. "My mother wasn't a wise lady," said the king. His gestures were valid, as what he said about his own mother weren't normal words.

"And Aarunya is none different than her grandmother," King added. Aarav didn't say anything, he waited for his father to continue. After a while king continued, "When your grandmother learned that gemstones hold irresistible power, the promise of immortality and eternal beauty, she went mad after them. I could see in her eyes, cravings to hold those gemstones as rings in her hand. Father passed on the responsibility of saving the ancestors to me. I wanted to awaken those gemstones for saving the ancestors, but she wanted to awaken the gemstones for immortality and eternal beauty. Her cravings were way more than mine. Then with time she started ageing, she felt that she won't be able to reap the benefits of gemstones, this is why she shared everything with Aarunya and gave her all those books. She did this because her life was either in Aarunya or in gemstones. She loved Aarunya more than gemstones," king uttered the truth, why he was not happy with the fact that Aarunya knows everything about the gemstones. "And Aarunya is on the same track," Aarav said. King nodded his head to give his consent in the statement of Aarav.

After a short pause, Aarav asked in impatience, "but father, why do mother consider all this evil, whatever you are doing. Why does she want gemstones not to be awakened?" For once king Mahendra didn't reply anything. Aarav waited for him to say something for a few seconds. When he didn't respond, Aarav again asked, "Are you also thinking of performing the dark magic which grandfather have performed." "No," king instantly replied. "Then why does mother consider that whatever you are doing is evil?" Aarav asked again in no time. "Even if I wanted to perform that dark magic then too I couldn't. The night when Sitara comet appears, has already passed," said king Mahendra, avoiding his son's question of why his mother considers all this evil.

After thinking for two seconds, Aarav said, "Probably you must be planning to do something more evil than what grandfather has done." "For now your knowledge about gemstones and process of awakening them is enough," said king Mahendra. Before Aarav could argue, they both heard their soldiers shouting outside, "Attack! Attack! King, it's an attack on us." Someone has attacked their troop.

6

The Selfish Servant

Aarunya was roaming here and there in her room. Her face had a sign of anxiety and hypertension. Her facial expressions were saying that something was bothering her deep down. The speed of her feet wasn't too fast and wasn't too slow. Her hands were twisting her dupatta. Thinking about something, her head was even sweating. Then while she was roaming around, Sahrindri entered her room. When Aarunya found Sahrindri in her room, she grumbled at her. "You made me do that dark magic. This all is happening because of you and your promises of eternal beauty and immortality," said Aarunya. "What is bothering you?" Sahrindri asked. "That old lady had asked me to kill someone I loved, remember?" "Yes, but why are you thinking of that black night again and again? I know you well, you will never kill someone you love, I know you," said Sahrindri.

Aarunya took another vertical round of her room. Her hands were again twisting her dupatta. Her forehead was still sweating. Her face's colour has turned pale and dull. It seemed as if she was hiding something and wasn't able to spit out the truth in front of even Sahrindri. Sahrindri was noticing her roaming in the room in anxiety.

This time Aarunya was roaming in the room hastily than before. It looked like she was in more tension after the arrival of Sahrindri, or she was in fear of sharing, what she was feeling. When Aarunya completed three vertical rounds of her room, Sahrindri asked, "What is that Aarunya?" Aarunya's back was visible to Sahrindri when she asked so. She was half done in her vertical round. After hearing her question, she stopped in between, turned around and came near to Sahrindri and said, "I am thinking to kill my own mother." she delivered those words in rage and anger. In anger, her eyes were looking deep in the eyes of Sahrindri and were asking why she took her to that old lady.

"What?" Sahrindri cried in reaction to the words of Aarunya. "I can't explain it to you, but from my inner self, I am getting this urge that if I kill my own mother, then I'll get irresistible powers and I am not being able to stop these thoughts of killing my own mother," Aarunya explained in details what was happening with her and why she was worried. "Relax! You are not going to do any such thing. I know," said Sahrindri. "Even I know that. But twenty-four hours a day I am getting the longings of killing my own mother. I am not able to change my thoughts. I don't know…. I don't know why these thoughts are controlling me. I am feeling so restless. It feels like I won't be calm until I'll do this," Aarunya shared all her happenings with Sahrindri.

History repeated itself in her family. The mistake which king Dharmendra made was repeated by his granddaughter, Aarunya. She performed the same dark magic and on the same night, which king Dharmendra had performed years ago. Although this time it was deceitfully performed by her, through Agastya but the fact was that Aarunya was suffering from same agony. The dark magic inside her was persuading her to kill someone she loved and attain power.

"If I had any idea about that this dark magic will be so futile and devilish for you then I would have never recommended it to you, trust me." Sahrindri said in her defense. She defended herself before Aarunya could accuse her more. "If you weren't my best friend then by now I would have had your head spiked on the wood of the same cemetery where you took me," said Aarunya in full anger. Her own best friend has put her in a situation where she had this urge and thoughts of killing her own mother. Her anger was all justified.

"Aarunya," Sahrindri cried her name. "Better start calling me princess and leave the room right now," princess Aarunya bawled at her. Sahrindri found it better to not to say anything and leave the room. Aarunya again started roaming in the room. Today she didn't have even time to stare at the coronet. She was feeling those great urges of killing her own other. Thus it was obvious that those instincts of her will bother her.

After leaving the room of Aarunya, Sahrindri left the palace too. Her steps moved toward the hill. Alone she headed towards the hill which was between the estate of Krishnapur and Indragadh. It was day time. That hill wasn't a short one, which could be crossed in just no time. Sahrindri looked here and there. She feared that someone might notice her. She then covered her face with her dupatta. She made a veil of it. In the peak summer, she started moving on the hill. Bright sunshine was tormenting her soft body, but she didn't give a damn to that sunshine, she kept on moving.

After moving for about fifteen minutes, she stopped. Her body wasn't allowing her to move further. She made herself sit on a rock. Yet she had not even covered one-fourth of the distance, and she had started panting heavily. Now, when she climbed a little bit of hill, she wasn't scared that someone might see her. This was because people of Krishnapur were settled down the hill. She uncovered her face from the veil. After a while, she again started moving. She was climbing the hill with all her strength. This time she started climbing the hill with more enthusiasm. She was determined no matter, how harsh the sun is burning, she will cross the hill anyhow.

She climbed the hill frantically for next twenty more minutes. This time she didn't take rest even for a minute. Probably she wanted to reach on time and return before sundown. She had crossed half the hill. Now she was standing on the top of hill. There she saw some soldiers of Krishnapur. They must be guarding the estate on its boundaries. Immediately, she put her veil again on her face. She hardly managed to go by hiding from those soldiers.

Climbing a hill up is way difficult than moving downside. When Sahrindri was moving down, her pace was doubled and neither did she take rest in between. She managed to hide from the soldiers of Indragadh too. In no time she crossed the hill. After crossing the hill, she was standing on the edge of Indragadh. Her eyes looked here and there for someone. She didn't move, perhaps she was looking for someone to come and take her.

She didn't have to wait for more. One man came near her and said, "Are you Sahrindri?" "Yes, how did you recognise me?" She asked. "From your attires, they didn't resemble to be of a lady from Indragadh." "Alright, where can I see Agastya?" Sahrindri asked. "Come with me." then she followed that person. He took him on her feet, no chariot or horse. Sahrindri had already crossed a big hill to come to Indragadh, she was exerted. Still, she had no choice but to move. He made her walk for another five minutes. Sahrindri could notice that he was talking her through a secret way.

They entered an old house, wherein its one room, Agastya was waiting for her. When Sahrindri entered inside, he said, "I hope you are here with good news. "Have I ever disappointed you?" said Sahrindri. Agastya devilishly smiled in response. "Dark magic that had entered inside Aarunya is performing well," said Sahrindri. "Is she getting those urges?" Agastya asked in excitement. "Yes, today itself she was grumbling at me that why did I take her to that old lady. She is feeling to kill her own mother and gain power. She confessed this in front of me," Sahrindri told him everything.

Agastya who was standing in front of her, went back and took out a pouch from one bag. He again came near Sahrindri and handed over to her. That bag contained golden coins. "Here is your reward," he said. Sahrindri looked at him angrily. Looking at the bag, she said, "This is not what was promised." Agastya kept silent. For another three-four seconds no one spoke. Then Sahrindri again opened her mouth to say, "I want to marry your son, a brahmin boy. This is what I have asked. I was born as a low born girl, I don't wanna die in the same state. I want prestige and honour for the rest of my life," said Sahrindri in another breathe.

Agastya took back the bag of gold coins from her, went back and placed it in the bag again. Then he turned towards her, this time he didn't come near her. "This is what you demanded at the time of the deal, I didn't promise that," he said, standing at a reasonable distance from her. "But you didn't deny it," said Sahrindri in a heavy voice. "But I didn't promise it either," Agastya replied with confidence on his face. Sahrindri stretched her eyes in anger and said, "You can't step back from it. You will have to marry me with your son." She had protest's tone in her words. She was demanding justice for her deal. She had fulfilled her part of duty by taking Aarunya to that old lady, and now she wanted Agastya to fulfil his part. "There is no such word like silent consent. Silent promises can never be trusted," said Agastya. "You cannot back off from your deal. You will have to fulfil your part," said Sahrindri.

After a while, Agastya said, "That's impossible Sahrindri." "Why? Is your son married? I am even ready to become the second wife of a brahmin boy," said Sahrindri immediately. In just one second she took the decision to become a second wife of a brahmin boy. This very well said how eager she was to change her low born identity. This also depicted that all the time in her life, she must have lived in inferiority. "Still that's not possible Sahrindri," Agastya said. "You haven't denied my offer when we made the deal, then why are you not ready now?" Sahrindri asked.

Agastya stayed silent for other five seconds. "Answer me," Sahrindri roared at him. "This is because I don't have a son. I am not even married," Agastya spit out truth in his next statement. "What….?" Sahrindri cried slowly. Then after a pause of five seconds, she went near him and yelled, "You ugly cunning brahmin. I will not spare you. I will tell everything to Aarunya about your plans, then instead of killing her mother, she'll kill herself. I'll destroy you," Sahrindri expressed her heart.

Agastya smiled and replied after one second, "Do you think a low born… inferior minded girl can even think to destroy me." "I will do that. Just wait and watch, I will not let you succeed in your mission with gemstones… never and ever" said Sahrindri and turned to walk out. Agastya immediately called two soldiers, they came from another room and grabbed

Sahrindri from her arms. When she tried to yell, another soldier covered her mouth with a piece of cloth. She tried to get rid of them. Her eyes were straight away looking at Agastya. She was moving up and down to get rid of them. The soldiers dragged her with her arms. Her legs were struggling to not to go with them. But all her efforts went to waste, they dragged her towards a room.

"*Person who can betray one, can betray anyone,*" said Agastya. He kept on seeing the soldiers pulling her into a room. He kept his continuous gawking eyes on them. Sahrindri kept fighting for freedom but she was trapped in between two muscular soldiers, her every effort to get freedom from them, ought to go waste. At last, they tied her hands and legs. They also tied her mouth, so that she could no longer shout. She, on the other hand, was still fighting for freedom. She was even trying to shout more and more. Her throat was choking. Those three soldiers shut the gate and locked the room. Agastya's eyes were still on them.

"No-one can come between me and my purpose with gemstones.... No-one," Agastya murmured with confidence to himself and left the room. A chariot was waiting outside that old home for Agastya. Agastya went ahead and sat in it. Then he ordered the chariot driver to move towards the palace.

Agastya went straight to the place where soldiers were practicing. They were planning an attack on the estate of Krishnapur, thus obviously they needed to be all prepared. Thousands of soldiers were practicing in the ground. Swords were playing with one another fiercely. Swords were attacking on one another like two lions were fighting with each other for their territory. Sometimes a slant right, sometimes a slant left or sometimes straight, swords were attacking one another constantly. The rattling of those swords seemed none less than a real war's noise. Every warrior was practicing like they were really fighting in battle-field. The practicing ground seemed none less than a battlefield. The gleaming blades of steel swords in the entire practicing ground were giving a fierce look.

Agastya was gazing at them with one continuous look. The warriors were actually practicing for Agastya and his goals. After all, the attack on Krishnapur was planned by Agastya only, and he was the one to sow the seeds of greed of marriage with princess Aarunya in king Ashoka's heart. Therefore, from every aspect, those soldiers were practicing in favour of Agastya, instead of king Ashoka.

He was standing in the corner. His one hand was touching his thigh, and another was carrying his brahmin dupatta with pride. His bald head and one thin brahmin ponytail was doing nothing but adding into his ugliness. He had an eagle's eye on the ground, very keenly he was observing them practicing. He felt a sense of vanity, seeing them practicing. Probably, he was seeing his dreams coming true in those practicing soldiers. His ears were continually hearing the sound made by hundreds of swords. He was seeing them without any expressions on his face. Like an idol, he was standing there.

From a complete view, he shifted his eyes to two soldiers practicing just near him. Their swords were moving left and right and were making noise for half a minute. Sometimes their swords went down the leg and sometimes not. Agastya noticed them for another half minute. Then he went near them. Soldiers got cautious when they found him noticing them. When they found Agastya's eyes on them, they became vigilant. They started putting more efforts into practice. But still, their act of performance didn't improve. Their swords were still moving sometimes left and right, and sometimes down the leg.

"Stop!" said Agastya in a harsh tone. Immediately their hands stopped, and both of them greeted him by lowering their down. "My lord!" They both said in one tone. "Are you fighting or playing with swords," said Agastya. Both of them looked at each other and then looked down. Agastya was rebuking them for their practice, they were ought to feel ashamed. They were boys of age around twenty or twenty-one. Agastya added, "You both are just defending, no-one among you is attacking. This way we are not gonna win the estate of Krishnapur." Both kept quite in his honour. Agastya was right on his point. He had been observing them for about a minute now. They couldn't even get the other one to loose. One minute in a battlefield is too long to survive. One needs to be present as a fighter on the battlefield, if he wants to survive then he needs to be all attentive.

After the instructions of Agastya, they again started practicing. Again swords started playing left, right and down. For another half minute, Agastya stared at them practicing with each other. But he could see no improvement. "Stop!" he again said to them. Both of them again stopped. They were again looking down. "Attack on one another's mind," said Agastya with no expressions on his face. Right after his instructions, they started practicing again. After fifteen seconds the right soldier attacked the waist of the left one. As and when his mind diverted to defend near the waist, the right soldier attacked near his knuckle and dropped his sword. Agastya gave no expressions on the better performance of the right soldier.

Then looking at the left soldier, he repeated his words, "Attack on the mind."

"Since when did brahmins started giving training on how to fight?" said the general of the army from behind. He had been noticing Agastya for quite some time before he opened his mouth He spoke as and when he found it convenient. Agastya turned back and gave him a look. Looking at him, in a second he figured it out that the general is still not happy with the decision of attack on Krishnapur. He gave an evil smile while looking at him. The chief of the army had pointed on his caste and his teachings, he was expecting Agastya might say something soon to him. Before Agastya's tongue, his evil smile and sharp looks talked with the chief of the army. He was saying that in the estate of Indragadh, he is none less than a king. Facial expressions of the chief of the army were saying that he is very well aware of the fact that Agastya is none less than a king. Still he is a lot more confident in his own domain and was disliking the intervention of Agastya in wars.

"The estate where they are preparing an attack is ruled by a brahmin emperor, so it's better if they would be guided by another brahmin," said Agastya. He was still maintaining his evil smile on his face. Chief of the army wasn't sagacious like him, he couldn't hide his feelings. His face was loudly speaking out that how unhappy he was with Agastya on his sudden decision to attack Krishnapur.

"They are my men. I treat them all like my children. I don't train them to one-day die for nothing," said the chief of the army. His eyebrows were twisted, and his forehead had curves. His tone was too harsh to talk with a person who was on the second position in the realm, after the king. He was resolutely blaming him of putting soldier's life on risk for nothing good. He had love and loyalty towards every common citizen who was part of his army.

Agastya for once wanted to say that they were Rajputs, they are born to fight and die for the kingdom. But he didn't say so, he wanted to spontaneously frame words which could justify his sudden decision of attack on the realm of Krishnapur. "They won't be fighting and dying for nothing. They would be all doing it for the interest of realm. King Ashoka will increase his territory, beyond the hill of Sarita river and our people will have full access to water of Sarita river," said Agastya. Though Agastya wasn't obligatory to give him any of such explanations, still he did, for he wanted to make sure that chief of army doesn't believe that the war is because of him.

"Our people do not have any shortage of water, and we do not need to expand our territory on the cost of lives of my innocent men," said the chief of the army. He again referred the soldiers of Indragadh as his men with proud. His love towards commoners was overflowing. "Then why do you train them, if you cannot make them fight for expanding territory? Do you just train them for defense, is this the true duty of a Rajput? A Rajput is born to fight for his realm, and all our soldiers are Rajputs or Kshatriya," Agastya again deceitfully delivered his words. That was rhetoric to say that do you just train them for defense.

This time chief of the army took few seconds to reply, probably he was thinking to again retort to Agastya with some better arguments. After a while, he said, "I agree that Rajputs and Kshatriyas are born to fight… but for realm… not for serving the selfish goals of an ugly brahmin." He attacked Agastya barefacedly. He even dared to call him ugly in front of his face. Agastya was like the right hand of king and king demanded respect for him by all citizens just equal to him. With the presence of all such facts, the chief of army dared to say so.

But Agastya wasn't a fool to react with resentment on him. He wanted to make sure that in any case, he shouldn't get an idea that the war was happening because of Agastya. "What makes you believe that an attack on a realm would personally benefit me? I am not even married; I don't crave gold from the king on victory. Even in future, I don't wanna marry any pretty princess of Krishnapur's brahmin royal family or anything else from Krishnapur. Then what you think, how the battle can benefit me?" Agastya countered him with his best possible thoughts. He made his context that how a poor unmarried brahmin can be benefited from a war between two realms.

The chief of army replied, "That I don't know, but I am just sure that you are cunning brahmin, who is mysterious and enigmatic and most importantly who cannot be trusted. King is nothing but your puppet." He dared to even abuse about the king in front of none but Agastya. He seemed an honest person by his attributes, who was bold enough to open his heart. "In your daring, you are crossing your limits," Agastya warned him that he was talking abusively about the king in front of him. "I am not a coward to speak out the truth," said the chief of the army and moved a bit away from Agastya. He shifted his eyes towards practicing soldiers.

At that moment king too arrived to have a look at the practicing soldiers. "Your Highness!" both Agastya and chief of army greeted king Ashoka. "So how are our men doing with swords?" King inquired. "They are doing quite well, but need to improve in certain things," said Agastya. When he delivered a critical comment about soldiers, chief of the army gave him a sceptical look. He wasn't liking that Agastya was commenting on men trained by him.

"We will not be visiting Krishnapur for a tour, we'll be attacking there. Our men need to improve soon," said the king. The coming war has sown the seeds of excitement in his heart too. He was eagerly waiting to win beautiful princess Aarunya in his palace and in his bedroom. He looked at the ground, where innocent soldiers were preparing to fight for their ruler. Soon their lives will be in danger just because the realm was feeding them two times bread and butter. Agastya was looking at Ashoka. He was seeing the grown-up tree of greed for a beautiful princess.

"Your Highness, have we informed the estate of Krishnapur about the attack," chief of the army said after a while. It seemed like a Scorpio had bitten king Ashoka. If he or Agastya speaks a lie that they have informed the realm of Krishnapur about the attack, then that lie will be revealed in the battlefield, when he'll find that king Mahendra and Aarav are absent in Krishnapur. On the next hand, if he'll utter the truth, then he will have to feel abashed in front of the chief of the army. King Ashoka instead of giving a reply to him, gave a look to Agastya. Chief of army noticed that the king and Agastya were blank on his question. It took him no time to understand that the attack was a surprise attack and it was all planned by Agastya. The look of Ashoka at Agastya was saying it all.

Agastya and Ashoka were wondering in their hearts that instead of informing Krishnapur estate about the attack, they were attacking them in the absence of their emperor. Both of them were pondering how the chief of army will react in the battlefield when he finds out that they have attacked in the absence of King Mahendra and his son Aarav.

"Your Highness, pardon me, but I am scared that we are taking a coward step of attacking without informing," said the chief of the army. Agastya had prepared himself to answer him. "A minute before you told me that your men aren't there to die for nothing. So it's not a coward but a brave step. We cannot put our men's life on risk for nothing. We have to make sure that if we are attacking, then we are winning. Commoners do not take birth just to die for the realm," Agastya countered him in his own words.

The chief of the army couldn't hide from his face that he hated Agastya more with every passing second. He turned towards the king and said, "Your Highness! I cannot win with Sir Agastya in words, but in my opinion, I will always suggest to inform and then attack." King was already in favour of Agastya. He was really his puppet in every sense. "I think Agastya is right, we cannot put our soldier's life on risk," like a perfect puppet, the king just repeated his words. "Whatever you think right my lord," said the chief of the army. King was Agastya's puppet, and other vital ministers were serving the king with their loyalty. This cycle only signified that the estate of Indragadh was ruled more or less by Agastya.

"Now let's have a look at our archers," said the king Ashoka. Three of them moved towards another ground where estate's archers were practicing. In another ground, archers were practicing. Hundreds of arrows were being released from the crossbow and were hitting the targets on the tree. Agastya and

Ashoka could notice that their archers weren't performing well like their swordsmen.

"I have heard that being a brahmin estate, Krishnapur have skilled archers and they are known to win battles because of their improvised archery," said the chief of the army. He was against the decision of battle, this is why he was demotivating king Ashoka and Agastya.

"*One loses a battle first with thoughts, not with swords*," said Agastya again to win over the chief of the army with his words. He continued, "Numerically our soldiers' strength is higher than the estate of Krishnapur. Moreover our swordsman are real fighters, there is no chance we will lose the battle against Krishnapur." "But archers can win the battle, without the numerical strength…," chief of army tried to argue with Agastya, but this time the king intervened, "Enough! The war is fixed… and we must think how to win, instead of thinking about our weaknesses." He made chief of army keep quiet for then. The chief of army tried his best till last to avoid the battle against Krishnapur, but he couldn't.

"We shall call a meeting to make a strategy for the coming war," said Agastya. Chief of army gazed him with his tough looks, as he uttered his dialogue. But in front of the king he decided not to counter him. "I am already up with a plan," said the chief of the army after a while. He probably wanted to flabbergast the king with his preparation, or maybe he really had a plan with him. "I think we all shall listen to your plan in a meeting with other ministers, they might give better suggestions or amendments." Said Agastya. Chief of army hated him more when he raised doubts on his plan. Agastya didn't mean to intentionally humiliate him. All that he wanted was to win the war at any cost, this is why he wanted the opinion of all.

While Agastya was countering the chief of the army, king Ashoka was still busy staring the archers. Since half a minute he was looking at them with a hawk's eye. "We are really weak at arching; we need to do something about it." He disliked the performance of archers in that half a minute. Agastya who was more worried than anyone else for the war, gazed at practicing archers. He too analysed them for a couple of seconds. "We will win the war from our swordsman, king," he murmured to himself. Maybe he was consoling himself about the victory.

"Let's move to the meeting room, I have already informed the other ministers," said the king. Then Agastya, king and chief of the army moved towards the meeting room. Other ministers were already waiting for the king. They all stood up to greet the king. King ordered with his hand to ministers to be seated, he was serious in his looks, plausibly he was worried about the archers.

"So what my ministers have planned so far about the war and its strategy?" said the king. He was expecting his intellectual ministers to come up with a plan for the upcoming war. Agastya was a brahmin, king wasn't expecting anything relating to war from him. For next four five seconds, nobody in the room uttered a word. Nobody was prepared for a sudden war.

"I think we must arrange archers in the first line of our army," said Agastya when nobody came up with any suggestions. "What?" King and chief of army cried. They both have witnessed that the estate of Indragadh was weak at arching and Agastya was talking to place archers on the first line. "Not even five minutes have passed, since we three witnessed that we are weak at arching, and great Agastya, king's mentor, wisdom holder is talking to place them on our first line," said the chief of the army. He couldn't miss a chance to humiliate him in front of the king and other ministers. "Suggesting about a war and making a strategy for it are different things altogether," said one of the minister. Their enviousness towards Agastya was talking in their words.

"I am also not really agreeing with you Agastya here, but still would like to listen why you are thinking so," said the king. King Ashoka had faith in him like anything, he wouldn't dare to question his thoughts and suggestions at first instance. Other ministers had to keep quiet, seeing king was still eager to listen to him. "Our enemies are known to have mastery at arching. When they see us coming for the attack, they will definitely place archers in their first line. We are good with our swordsman, but sitting on horses and on a distance they cannot fight with archers. To demonstrate their talent, they'll have to go near them, but archers will demonstrate their talent from a distance. Thus, we cannot expect our swordsman to stand on the first line and die for nothing….," Chief of army cut him short, "So you mean we are going to wilfully sacrifice our archers so that our swordsman can further demonstrate their talent and can bring us the colourful victory."

Agastya was only thinking about winning the war at any cost, he wasn't giving thoughts to ifs and buts of winning the war. This is why he suggested that instead of sacrificing their best men, better sacrifice the weaker ones. Chief of the army on the other hand was concerned towards the soldiers, whom he had personally trained. He didn't have any greed of winning the battle, but had concern towards his soldiers.

When the chief of army made his squabble on Agastya's idea of placing archers on first line, Agastya in another second replied, "Do we have any other option?" He was unabashed in talking about options, he didn't care about the lives of soldiers of his own realm. "You are talking to directly kill our archers in the name of war," said the chief of army. "I am not agreeing with you chief. It's a war and soldiers are going to die anyhow. Understand Agastya's strategy behind it. Our first line ought to be sacrificed, then instead of getting our swordsman killing, we must sacrifice our archers. Moreover, our archers will lay the platform for our swordsman. It's a surprise attack, thus Krishnapur won'thave plenty arrows prepared with them, we'll slay them easily," the king made his point. He understood Agastya's game plan very well.

"We win wars more by the brain, rather with swords or arches," said Agastya when king in a sense applauded his strategy. The Chief of the army and other envious ministers couldn't say anything against the king. The Chief of the army was still loathing the fact that the archers were being intentionally sacrificed, and he didn't have any other valid argument to lay.

"Does anyone else has a better plan?" king asked. Ministers were still quite. The sudden war gave them no chance to come up with something brilliant so soon. "I think we must also think something about the river. The way we are gonna fight near river will decide our victory," said Agastya. Agastya sounded more like a warrior than a brahmin while talking about strategy of war. "When over the hill, soldiers of Krishnapur will see us, they'll, first of all, send their archers to fight. If we are placing our archers on the first line, then I think we must send a fraction of our best swordsman near the river because their swordsman will be weakest," said the chief of the army.

In just another second Agastya said, "Completely agree with you over this." He wasn't in any competition with the chief of the army or any other ministers, he was clear in his goals; to win the war at any cost. Therefore, he was supporting the chief of the army when he was right in his context. "Here you have my consent too," said king Ashoka to grant permission over chief's suggestion.

"Your highness you can take charge of King Mahendra, and I'll take care of Aarav," said the chief of the army after a while. When he said so, both king and Agastya instantly made eye contacts. In just a fraction of second, they looked at the other side. They never wanted to disclose the fact that they were aware of the absence of King Mahendra and Aarav while attacking the realm of Krishnapur.

"One more important thing we need to be aware of is that the castle of Krishnapur is a moated castle. Are we…," Agastya tried to make one point. "I know that. I have already informed, and trained soldiers to how to enter inside the castle," chief of army cut him short. He left no chance to counter Agastya. Agastya smiled and said, "That's good." In his heart chief of the army was still concerned about the lives of his soldiers, but all that he could do was to obey the orders of King Ashoka who was obeying the orders of Agastya.

Then the meeting discussed other aspects of the war. Then Agastya said, "I'll also be joining the war with weapons." He dropped a bombshell over the ministers and even the king. So far he hasn't fought in any war in the eyes of the king and other ministers, and this would be the first time he'll be joining any war, according to them. Thus, they were expected to act in surprise.

"But Agastya...," said the king, before anyone else could counter him. Agastya cut him short, "It has been only three years, since I joined your ministry, after the death of my father. I have knowledge of arms and weapons from my past life, you don't know about it." "But I have never seen you fighting you in any war before this one," said king Ashoka. "That's a brahmin empire, we are fighting, so better take a brahmin with us to face them," said the chief of the army. Chief of the army wasn't pleased with Agastya that he was putting innocent soldier's life on stake, thus he was happy with Agastya's decision that he was ready to face the possibility of death in front of him. Other ministers too didn't oppose his statement.

"I don't want to lose you. You are the gem of my realm," said the king with emotions. The king who was almost sure about his victory wasn't sure that whether his brilliant Agastya can survive on the battlefield or not. "You will not," said Agastya with pride and confidence in his voice. "Alright! As you think fit," said the king to deliver his statement of consent. He agreed because he had confidence in Agastya that any of his decision won't be without any cause, and will definitely favour the war.

7

The Cursed Tribe

Both Aarav and king Mahendra took out the sword. The words that reached their ears were, 'Attack! Attack on us!' They were lost talking about their gemstones and grandparents of Aarav. Abrupt attack on their troop bought them back into the present. In less than a second, they went out of the tent, with their swords ready to attack the neck of foe. But what they saw outside, was beyond their imagination. When they heard of the attack, all they could imagine was some burglars attacking troop in greed of pearls that royal people might be carring on their bodies. More than they could imagine was some rivalry kingdom might have attacked them, without warning. But there was something different, which their eyes witnessed right after they went out.

There were five creatures, whose half body was of human and half was hairy like a wolf. Even their face was half of human and half of wolf. They were standing and fighting like a normal human, with their hands. Their height was slightly more than a normal human being, and their body physic was definitely more than a normal human being. In half human and half animal's body, they had broadened chest and muscles of an obstinate warrior. Like any other human, they too had swords in their hands. Their fighting skills with swords were none less than the soldiers of the troop of King Mahendra.

They were only five and King Mahendra's troop had not less than fifteen soldiers who were fighting against those creatures. Still, in just one glance they could figure out that their enemy was weighing more than their men in the battlefield. To handle one among them, three soldiers were struggling, they were so good at using swords against them. Soul of Aarav and king Mahendra felt petrified when they saw them. Their body shivered like they were being placed on an iceberg. Had there been a normal human attack, they would have handled easily and would have not been petrified like hell.

But it wasn't the time to stand stagnant and watch the fight. After just two seconds, when king Mahendra and Aarav were done analysing the personality of their enemy, both jumped in the battlefield, to aid their soldiers.

One creature among them attacked the hand of one of the soldier with a sword. His sword dropped, and his hand started bleeding, he gave up fighting against him. That creature hastily caught the sword and threw it in the bushes. The other two soldiers were trying to harm his body continually but were failing, he was so good in defending himself from the attack. When the soldier with one bleeding hand gave up fighting, in that very moment Aarav joined the other two to attack him. He made the right choice to attack that creature who had just made one soldier armless. Aarav made his first attack on his waist. He was relatively short to attack straight on the creature's neck. The creature's waist started bleeding. The creature was yet busy fighting with the other two soldiers. He didn't pay attention to his bleeding waist. His right hand was busy performing his sword against the two soldiers. It seemed like three people were struggling to fight against him. One soldier was already gone and was replaced by Aarav, who made no difference.

King Mahendra too had joined another group of three soldiers, fighting against one creature. He was skilled more than his son in handling the sword. Clearly, when he joined, he made the creature struggle more. By now that creature was defending himself sharply, but when King Mahendra started fighting against him, he started to struggle more. King Mahendra gave him two-three injuries on his waist and back. But King Mahendra too was unsuccessful in attacking his neck and lessening at least one of the five unidentified enemies.

In the other three group of fighters, the creatures were on winning side. The soldiers of King Mahendra were struggling against them. They were attacking from swords brilliantly. Handling three swords with one sword seemed their left hand's task. But one thing was ambiguous in their fighting. It was flawless that they were far better in fighting than the soldiers of King Mahendra. Still none among them were attempting to kill any one of them. No matter how many times king Mahendra, Aarav and their soldiers were trying to attack their neck and kill them, but those five creatures weren't trying to kill any one of them.

When fighting became boring for one of them, that creature threw the soldier behind the bushed with a single push of the hand. One soldier was injured and was thrown in between the thorny bushes, making both of them armless and helpless to fight more against them. The one who had thrown one of them behind the bushes became more violent. Now he was fighting with only two soldiers. Thus it was easier for him to handle them.

Aarav and his group of soldiers went inside the tent while fighting. Aarav was a good swordsman; he was handling him smarter than his soldiers. When they were fighting inside the tent, that creature tore the cloth of tent from one of his hand. He did that act most probably in frustration and anger.

Looking at the torn piece of cloth, Aarav got an idea. He made himself distant from the fighting for a moment. He left the creature with the other two soldiers and went near the torn piece of cloth.

In no time he took the stool on which he and his father were sitting a few minutes before. He then took the piece of cloth and climbed on the stool. When the creature was busy fighting with the two soldiers, he wrapped the piece of cloth around the neck of that creature and tried to press his neck with all his pressure. When Aarav did so, creature yelled. For the first time, they heard the voice of that creature. It was a human sound. That made them more perplexed about them. Their appearance was of a beast, and the way they yelled was similar to human. The other two soldiers started attacking his beast-like body brutally. He was still struggling to fight and survive. Still, soldiers couldn't kill him, only the pressure of Aarav on his neck was making him helpless.

By now that vicious creatures who had thrown one of the soldiers in between the thorny bushes got free from the other two soldiers too. When he heard the voice from inside the tent, he straight away went inside the tent. Looking at Aarav, who was trying to kill one of his mates, he went near him and pulled him from his back. He then took the same cloth and tied Aarav's hands, with it.

Now inside the tent, there were two soldiers and two creatures. By now they had gotten the idea to tie them with the piece of cloth of tent. It took them just another five to six seconds to tie the other two soldiers with Aarav with the same piece of cloth. Those soldiers couldn't do anything for their defence. It was now more clear that creatures had no intention of killing them or even harming them.

After tying Aarav and the two soldiers, the two creatures came out of the tent. The remaining three creatures had made king Mahendra harmless by then. After tying Aarav and two soldiers inside the tent, they attacked the group outside. When they were five, they were hard to handle by fifteen soldiers, King Mahendra and Aarav. It took them no time to make all of them harmless and helpless in front of them. It was still hard to believe that despite being beasts by their physical appearance, their intention wasn't to kill any of them.

The five creatures then easily managed to tie even King Mahendra and remaining soldiers with the help of cloth of the tent. It was hard to understand how those beasts got that brain to tie all of them by tearing the cloth of tent. The great king Mahendra and his son were helpless. After tying all of them, those creatures started collecting jewellery that king Mahendra, Aarav had on their bodies. They took every garland, every pearl in fingers or ears and every possible ornament on any of them. They searched everywhere and when they were satisfied that nothing is left on their bodies or anywhere else, they left the place without untying them. They ran back to the forest, probably to the one where they came from.

Emperor Mahendra was tied with his hands and was helpless to help his people and son. When those creatures were gone, king Mahendra, Aarav and all other soldiers started trying to open up their knots. King Mahendra luckily had a knife wrapped around his back. With the help of that knife, he cut the knot from his hands. After getting free, he untied the knots of Aarav and other soldiers too. All of them were slightly injured. They were smart enough to carry first aid medicines with them. Though this attack wasn't expected by any one of them, but an attack by other realms was expected. Thus, they carried the first aid medicines with them.

"What was that father?" said Aarav. "Even I am pondering the same question," said King Mahendra while dressing his wounds. "Those were creatures from the cursed tribe," said one of the soldier. Then every eye went on him, for he had answered the most tempting question. No one was expecting that anybody would answer, but still, if someone spoke something, that too was a matter of question. He referred them creatures from the cursed tribe. He used the word, 'cursed,' for them.

When that soldier found that every eye was looking on him, he felt the need to further explain. "My wife is from a nearby village, she told me about them," he said. "What you mean by cursed tribe?" asked Aarav. "There is an entire tribe like these creatures which is supposedly living in these forests since years. They are trying to find a cure for their curse," he added. "Curse means their half beast's body, right?" asked King Mahendra. "Yeah," he replied. "But why did they take our ornaments?" Asked one of the soldiers.

Everyone's eyes were on the soldier whose wife was from the nearby village. Every eye was looking for an answer. "They never trade them. They are beasts who do not crave for gold. The villagers speculate that they are looking for a cure. It is just a speculation, no one knows what they want," said that soldier. "But how can you say that there is an entire tribe of such kind of beasts?" Aarav asked. "That is also speculation," the soldier replied. "They look like beasts, but by heart they aren't," Aarav added. He was right in his context, for if those creatures wanted they could have killed all of them easily, but they didn't. They just took the ornaments and went.

"Father I want some time alone with you," Aarav demanded. The soldiers understood and left them in peace. Now that the tent was torn the soldiers made groups and went far from them. "What's the matter?" asked King Mahendra. "Are you not thinking what I am thinking?" said Aarav. King Mahendra look at him perplexed. He wasn't getting the context that Aarav was mentioning.

Aarav was standing at a distance from him, he went near him and whispered in his ears, "Don't you think that the cure which that cursed tribe is looking for is in the gemstones which we have with us." King Mahendra's eyes didn't show surprise on his statement. The very next moment king Mahendra got the point, why Aarav was saying so. Those creatures from the cursed tribe have stolen only the ornaments and looking at them there was no fair chance that they might be in greed of precious stones or gold. The villagers were right in their speculation that their greed was in getting the cure for their cursed body and cursed life.

After a pause, King Mahendra replied, "Yes, maybe you are right." "Father promise me that after awakening gemstones and after saving ancestors, we'll try to save the cursed tribe too," said Aarav with emotions. "I respect the empathy you have for the cursed tribe but our many generations have been trying to awaken those gemstones and terribly failing. How are you so sure that we'll be able to awaken the gemstones and save our ancestors?" said King Mahendra. His tone said, he was sad that he couldn't save his ancestors so far and was worried whether he could do that now or not. "I hope for best, I am just taking a promise from you that if we succeed in awakening the gemstones, then we'll help the cursed tribe too," Aarav said. "Yes, we will. Even I want to," king Mahendra assured. "*A leader who holds empathy for all never fails to rule longer*," he added.

When they were done talking, they called the other soldiers. "Now let's move. We are barely two hours distant from the palace of Ratnagadh," King Mahendra ordered. Soldiers got the horses ready and then they all again started moving towards the palace of Ratnagadh.

While moving, one of the soldiers asked, "Your Highness! Have we informed the king Vashisth, that we are coming to see them?" "That is not your concern," King Mahendra shut him up the very next moment. Nobody except the royal families of Krishnapur was aware of the gemstones. Thus, every step was taken ingeniously.

The two hours' journey came to an end, and soon king Mahendra, Aarav and their soldiers were outside of the palace of Ratnagadh. They were first stopped by the watchman outside the palace. When king Vashisth was informed about their arrival, he came with his queen to welcome them inside. King Vashisth hugged King Mahendra warmly. Looking at the queen, Mahendra smiled. Aarav found that smile unusual.

"Welcome, my friend," said king Vashisth. King Mahendra and King Vashisth shared a warm hug. They all sat in a royal room of the palace of Ratnagadh and had some formal talks.

It was night time when they reached the palace of Ratnagadh. Suitable royal arrangements were made for their rest. Aarav wanted to ask king Mahendra about the smile Mahendra exchanged with the queen of Ratnagadh but wasn't getting the right words to ask. Ignoring that he slept peacefully. In the middle of night, King Mahendra got up and left his room. After coming out of the guest room, he straight away went to the backyard of the palace where the queen of Ratnagadh was waiting for him alone. Mahendra had covered his face with a piece of cloth, but the queen of Ratnagadh wasn't scared of anyone, she had not covered her face with anything.

8

Innocent Servant of Agastya

"Eat something, else you'll die rotting here," said one of Agastya's servant to Sahrindri, who was captured in a room. It had been a day since Sahrindri was captured in the room. One servant of around twenty-twenty two years was there to keep an eye on her. Sahrindri was also of the same age. She was married in the city of Krishnapur and belonged from barista village, which came under the realm of Krishnapur.

"I'll prefer dying instead of eating the grains of an ugly fraud brahmin," said Sahrindri and took off her eyes from the servant. She was tied by legs and hands; she was lying on the floor. She started looking idly on the wall. "Look, who is talking about being fraud, one who betrayed her own queen and one who was about to betray her husband," said the servant. Sahrindri looked at him again. Her face didn't have any expressions. She gawked him for a few seconds idly, then again shifted her eyes idly on the wall. She completely ignored his taunt. "Lord Agastya haven't done any fraud with you. You are getting what you deserve," he added. His loyalty towards Agastya was bawling in his words. Sahrindri still ignored him, her eyes were still fixated on the wall.

"No one is coming to rescue you, so what's the point of dying of hunger," said the servant. "It's still a better option than to live a life where you are constantly reminded of your lower caste," she whispered. The servant smiled and started eating the food he was offering to her. "I am also a low born, but I never feel that I am deprived of my identity. Why you are so obsessed with marrying a brahmin boy?" said the servant.

"Even marrying a Rajput or Kshatriya will work," he again murmured softly.

"So your lord Agastya have offered his prisoner the same food which he offers to his servants. Is it my privilege or your shame?" said Sahrindri after a while. "It seems you have learned the art of words from lord Agastya," the servant said. "I have barely met two-three times with your lord Agastya," said Sahrindri in conceit, to prove the servant that she hasn't learned the art of words from anyone.

When the servant was done eating, Sahrindri asked, "What's your name?" "And why are you interested in knowing that? "the servant asked. "For sure, I am not interested because I am in love with you," said Sahrindri with arrogance in her tone. "So even prisoners can have sarcasm in their tone," the servant replied. Sahrindri found better not to reply. Her ignorance and arrogance in attitude were tempting the servant more to talk with her.

After a pause, he said, "I am Vishnu." Sahrindri who was looking at the wall, looked at him and said, "Nice knowing you Vishnu." She then shifted her eyes back to the wall. "So your husband never loved you or what?" Vishnu asked. She tilted her neck towards him. Her eyes were saying that she wasn't interested in talking with him. She again stared him for a few seconds and then she turned her neck back to the wall, without replying to him.

Vishnu was the only servant there to keep an eye on her. He was free to talk with her, he had no other job to do. More Sahrindri was ignoring him, more he was becoming curious to talk with her. Vishnu was still waiting for her to answer whether her husband loved her or not, but Sahrindri was rather busy in scrutinizing the wall.

"If you always wanted to marry a high caste boy then why did you marry a lower caste boy," said Vishnu again. He was a sweet boy who was just curious to know why a lady would betray her husband. "Because my parents forced me to," Sahrindri yelled at him. Her voice raised in anger and frustration. "Fine if you don't wanna talk," said Vishnu and proceeded to leave the room.

Before he could exit, Sahrindri said, "Listen!" Vishnu stopped on the doorsill, he looked back at her. Her face had arrogance. With same attitude, she said, "My husband loved me a lot. Still I decided to betray him. I left a letter for him asking him to never look for me." She was all forthright to accept the fact that despite having a loving husband, she decided to betray him.

Vishnu froze looking at the shameless version of her. Sahrindri looked pretty and innocent by face, in the corner of his heart Vishnu pitied for her. But when she became brazen in telling the truth that she had betrayed her loving husband, Vishnu's eyes wondered how a loving face's owner could be so selfish by heart.

"You are…," Vishnu tried to say something. "*Yes, I am selfish, and I am not ashamed of that,*" Sahrindri cut him short. Vishnu was an innocent boy who pitied the prisoned girl, when he found her so brutal, his heart couldn't collect words to say anything, for next five seconds. No one among them spoke anything. Vishnu was still standing on the doorsill.

After a while, Sahrindri added, "*We all are selfish, we all think about pleasing our self. Some try to please themselves by loving others, and some are bold enough to love just themselves.*" "How can you sleep with such thoughts?" Vishnu asked. Sahrindri closed her eyes, stretched her eyebrows and replied, "Peacefully."

Vishnu crossed the room. Sahrindri yelled, "Hey! I am now in mood to eat. Bring me some food." Vishnu gave furious looks at her, but unlike Sahrindri, he was good by heart. Moreover, he was asked by his master to keep an eye on Sahrindri, which included taking care of her food and other things too. Thus, being a loyal servant he bought the food for her.

"How I am gonna eat with tied hands," she asked. Then Vishnu tied her one hand with the pillar and kept an eye on her while she was eating. When she was done with the food, she asked, "I wanna pee." Vishnu untied her hands and legs then with a sword in his hand, he showed her the way to toilet. After peeing, when she came out, she said, "You'll be with me for twenty-four hours, what if you fall in love with me?" Vishnu replied, "I will never fall in love with a selfish person like you." "Let's see," said Sahrindri with a constant look on Vishnu.

At the palace of Krishnapur Aarunya's anxiety was on the peak when she found Sahrindri was missing. She was already fighting with herself, to not to kill her own mother and in that situation and now the girl who pushed her in this anxiety was missing. Aarunya ordered her soldiers to look for her best friend.

9

Hidden Relations

"Cover your face, what if someone sees us?" said king Mahendra. "I am not afraid of anyone, and you know why," the queen replied. Mahendra smiled and said, "That's your greatest advantage." The Queen of Ratnagadh and king Mahendra kept silent for another few seconds. Their eyes were fixed on each other's faces. After a while King Mahendra said, "how have you been Vichitra?" Queen smiled and after a suitable pause replied, "I am good! How about you?" Taking a deep breath, king Mahendra replied, "I am good too. How are your daughter and son?" He asked another question. "Chitrangna is good as well, and Chitrang isn't in the palace queen answered. "Why Chitrang does not live here? Have you triggered his….," Queen cut him short? "I don't wanna talk about my son ever…. Ever again." Mahendra had to accept her demand. He decided not to talk about her son ever again.

Then again for a couple of seconds, they glared each other. "We can sit somewhere and talk, my 'loyal ones' will take care that nobody should disturb us, while we are talking," said the queen. Then king Mahendra and queen Vichitra sat on a rock.

After a while king said, "A strange thing happened with us, when we were on the way to Ratnagadh." "And what's that?" "Five creatures attacked our troop," the King replied. Vichitra's eyes widened in wonder, she found it difficult to understand how someone could attack in a place known to her. "What kind of creatures?" She asked. The word creature made this clear that the attack wasn't by any kingdom or royal people. King Mahendra's face still had terror on his face, when he was imagining about those creatures.

Before Mahendra could answer her, she again asked, "Are you alright? They might have hurt you." "No, I am fine. it's just a few cuts that I got while fighting them," Mahendra consoled her. "Then why did they attack and what kind of creatures are you talking about," she fired a series of questions. "They were slightly taller than us, and half of their bodies was of wolf and remaining was of a human. They attacked us not to kill us, but just to take away our ornaments and jewellery." "I have never heard of such creatures in my life whose half body is of a wolf, and if they were such creatures then what are they going do with ornaments and jewellery," Vichitra asked logical questions.

Taking a sigh and a second's pause, Mahendra replied, "one of the soldiers from our troop told us that those creatures were from the cursed tribe and were looking for the cure for their bodies…," Mahendra tried to explain, but before he could complete, Vichitra cut him short. "…So you mean they wanted the gemstones." Mahendra sighed and answered, "Yeah! I think so. Only our gemstones could be powerful enough to give them cure of their cursed bodies."

The Queen didn't say anything after that. Probably she was worried about the gemstones. Mahendra added, "I have promised Aarav that we'll try to help the cursed tribe too when we are done with our purpose from gemstones." "What the hell, you told Aarav too about gemstones. Your daughter Aarunya is already aware about gemstones and now you told your son about as well," Vichitra grumbled at king Mahendra.

Before Mahendra could say something in his defence, she continued "You and I, we both have to save our ancestors. We can't put the gemstones at risk by telling everyone about them." King Mahendra gave tough looks at queen and said, "Aarav is not everyone." "I understand he is your son, but we should keep in our mind that we need to save ancestors, whose soul is trapped in those gemstones since years. We need to end their pain," Vichitra made her point. "I have also made my mind to help the cursed tribe after accomplishing our purpose with gemstones," said King Mahendra. "You shouldn't have told your son. He is too young to know about gemstones," Vichitra said, she didn't pay attention to helping the cursed tribe. She was so lost in her thoughts about the safety of gemstones.

She was looking down, Mahendra tilted her face toward him. Then looking in her eyes, Mahendra asked, "Let's not talk about my son. Tell me about your daughter, is she ready? Have you told her about gemstones and ancestors?" Vichitra, who was yet looking in Mahendra's eyes, disconnected eye contact with him and replied, "No, not yet." "What? Then what are you waiting for? We need to perform the dark magic on her as soon as possible. She will be the one to awaken those gemstones. You have given her birth, for this purpose only," said Mahendra. "I am not a fool, even I want to save ancestors more than you. But I want to know why you denied to perform the magic on Sitara night," Vichitra asked.

King Mahendra who was sitting on the rock beside Vichitra stood up, went little ahead and folded his hands. Vichitra was waiting for him to answer. "Speak up!" queen ordered. "Sources told me that Sitara comet night lessens the power. People perform that dark magic on Sitara night, to lessen the devil that enters inside you during that magic. Sitara night is considered as pure," said Mahendra. Vichitra stood up, went near Mahendra and said, "So you want dark powers to influence more on my daughter, Chitrangna." The Queen's voice said that she wasn't eventually happy with Mahendra's decision.

King Mahendra turned towards the queen and said, "I am doing all this to save ancestors… understand." The Queen remained silent for next three-four seconds. Then she moved closer to king Mahendra. King Mahendra gently placed his lips on hers. For five seconds, they remained in the same position. "I will take care of your daughter like mine," said Mahendra and hugged her. Then he relieved her and said, "I have missed you so much." Vichitra smiled and said, "Goodbye. Will see you tomorrow. I'll get the things ready as per our plan." She then disappeared from Mahendra's eyes in just a second. A few seconds before she was in front of him and in just another second she was gone. She magically vanished in just a second. Mahendra wasn't surprised at her magical disappearance. He stood there for half a minute idly and then left. When he entered in the room, Aarav asked, "Father, where you have been?" king Mahendra looked in his eyes and said, "I went to move one step ahead to awaken the gemstones." Before Aarav could further ask questions, where and why, Mahendra slept and said, "Good night."

While sleeping king Mahendra drowned in the thoughts of past. Thoughts of him and Vichitra.

10

Sahrindri's Move

Sahrindri was looking at Vishnu continuously. Sahrindri was sitting on the floor, with her hands and legs tied and Vishnu was sitting on a chair, placed at a distance of five feet from her. A minute passed in the same position Sahrindri was gazing at him and he was avoiding eye contact with her. "Will you stop looking at me like that," he, at last, had to say those words. "Like what?" Sahrindri asked and smirked. "Like that," Vishnu repeated his words. Poor lad couldn't collect words to define her that how she was making him uncomfortable with those looks. "Like what," Sahrindri too repeated her words. Maddened Vishnu got up from the chair and said, "I can keep an eye on you even while sitting outside too."

He was about to leave when Sahrindri yelled with egotism in her voice, "Fine! Fine! I am looking away." Vishnu gawked her with anger and sat back on his seat. Sahrindri had tilted her neck towards the wall. After half a minute she looked back towards him, providentially she found him looking at her. "Will you stop looking at me like that," said Sahrindri with a smile on her face. Instead of arguing with her further, Vishnu found it convenient to take off eyes from her immediately.

Sahrindri laughed loud to mock him. Vishnu looked at her with hatred and said, "What was so funny in that?" To reply him Sahrindri laughed louder. Vishnu got up to leave the room. "I am not that bad, the world made me so," Sahrindri whispered. Vishnu who was standing on the gate looked at her and said, "*World is same for all, it's we who decide whether to be good or bad… not world*" On his comeback Sahrindri smiled and said, "Ahmm… Seems like Agastya has great influence on you." "*I again accept that I am shamelessly selfish. For my benefit of a hundred bucks, I can make someone else's loss of hundred thousand bucks*," she added and smirked again while giving killing looks at him.

Vishnu ignored her and proceeded to leave the room. "I need a glass of water," she yelled from behind. By now Vishnu had crossed the room, he looked back towards her with irritation. She couldn't hide the devilish smile from her face, her smile and eyes accepted that she was just teasing him. When she found Vishnu continually looking at her with furious eyes, she said, "What? I really need water. I am feeling choked from the throat, because I just can't stop laughing at you," she said and burst out in laughter again.

Vishnu glared at her for few seconds and then left. Sahrindri was laughing with her heart. Her eyes were closed, and eyebrows tried to meet each other, while she was laughing at him. When she was done laughing at him, she opened her eyes. She saw a glass of water right in front of her face. Vishnu was holding the glass of water for her. She gazed his face for a while. For the first time, she had a different feeling for him, other than laughing and mocking him.

They kept looking at each other's face for three seconds. After that, Vishnu realised that she cannot drink water with tied hands. He kept the glass on the floor, checked on his sword and then started opening her tied hands. "Why so much of efforts for making me drink just a glass of water, when you can make me drink," said Sahrindri with sarcasm in her tone. Vishnu looked at her. "By your own hands," she added, and this time she had lust in her voice.

Vishnu again ignored her and opened her tied hands completely. Then he placed his right hand on his sword. When

Sahrindri found him, checking on his sword, she said, "Why are you checking on your sword again and again. Don't worry at all. I am not absconding from here without you." She then winked at him. Vishnu firmed his grip on his sword and said, "You have five seconds to empty that glass of water down your throat," Vishnu ordered to make her sure that she is the prisoner and he is the keeper. So, she cannot dominate him after a level.

"Alright! Alright!" said Sahrindri and took the glass of water in her hand. While looking at Vishnu with lusty looks, she placed her lips on the glass lusciously. Slowly she gulped the water with her relentless looks on Vishnu. Vishnu too maintained boring and dull eye contact with her, till the time she was drinking the glass of water. When she was done, he snatched the glass and again tied her hands.

He then proceeded to leave the room. She again yelled from behind, "I wanna pee." She was playing with him. When Vishnu looked back at her, she was smirking. She again couldn't hide her devilish smile from her face. Vishnu kept staring at her for few seconds. He had signs of anger and irritation on his face. "What? My digestive system is too fast. The moment I drink k water, it finds its way to come out," she said with her devilish smile. Vishnu went near her, untied her knots and on the tip of his sword he took her to the washroom. While standing outside the gate of the toilet, Sahrindri winked and said, "wanna come inside." On listening, this Vishnu pushed her inside and closed the door.

When she came out, he again tied her legs and hands. Then instead of going out, he went and again sat on his chair. "Seems like someone is literally interested in sitting here to stare me," said Sahrindri because Vishnu was supposed to leave her alone and sit outside the room. "I wanted to know what wrong the world has done to you, which made you so selfish," said Vishnu.

Sahrindri smiled and said, "What if you fall in love with me after hearing my part of the story." Instead of denying Vishnu replied, "We'll figure out that later." Sahrindri looked at him for a few seconds and asked, "What's that?" "What" Vishnu couldn't understand what she was asking. "Those looks of yours depicts that you are interested in me," she replied. When Vishnu took interest in Sahrindri's story, that made it clear that there is something which Vishnu might have started liking in her. Vishnu smiled and said, "Maybe your honesty drives me more."

Sahrindri smirked, took a noticeable pause and then asked, "How old are you?" Vishnu blinked his eyes and moved his eyebrows in her sudden question and then replied, "twenty-one… why you asked so... out of the blue." Looking straight in his eyes, Sahrindri replied, "Nothing…," then after a short pause added, "*Some people are too innocent to survive in the cruel world for long.*" Sahrindri referred Vishnu innocent, instead of paying attention to that Vishnu again asked, "Now will you speak up." Again for no reason, Sahrindri glared him continuously for a couple of seconds and then said, "You said the world is the same for all… would like to listen to yours first. Let's kill time by listening to each other's story."

Vishnu got up from the chair. Then he took the chair in his hand and placed near Sahrindri. "Wanted to see me from near?" said Sahrindri in her flirting tone. She had those expressions on her face when she said so. "Yes, because I wanted to look deep in those selfish eyes and tell them that I had to bear a lot more than you, still I didn't choose to betray anyone in my life," Vishnu said to her while looking straight in her eyes. Again unabashedly Sahrindri smiled and said, "How many times you want to hear from me that yes I am selfish and I am not ashamed of that."

Vishnu thought that maybe by telling her his story, he could change her. Again while looking in her eyes, he started reciting his story. "I do not belong from Indragadh." When he said so Sahrindri's eyes widened in wonder, as she couldn't believe that even being Agastya's servant, he does not belong to Indragadh. "Even lord Agastya does not belong from Indragadh," he added. "What?" Sahrindri couldn't control the word, 'what' from coming out from her mouth.

Now she got more interest in his story than before. "Then where is he from?" She asked. Instead of knowing from where does Vishnu belongs, she was more concerned from where does Agastya belong. "We both are from Dwarka," Vishnu replied. "The city located near the ocean," said Sahrindri. "Yes… ten days distant from Indragadh," Vishnu added. "So is that your part of the story that you belonged from another city and came here," Sahrindri rudely asked before Vishnu could complete.

Vishnu sighed and said, "Are you going to listen to me or draw your own conclusions." "Alright! Spit it up." "My father was a stableman in the realm of Dwarka. He could barely feed us two times bread. I was four when my biological mother died. Then my father remarried when I was five. I don't have words to define, how cruel my stepmother was to me. She made me do all household chores at the age of five. Then she forced my father to make me work as a stable boy with him so that I can earn and give few pennies to her. I was bullied by other stable boys who were elder than me. Once when I was working, a boy indulged in a fight with me. I was avoiding to fight with him. He pushed me on the floor, my mouth started bleeding. It was then when lord Agastya saw me. Then he punished that boy… after that, he took me with him. After meeting lord Agastya, I never saw my father and stepmother. Then before three years, he took me to the realm of Indragadh. He is everything to me. He treats me like his own son." Vishnu uncovered everything he had in his heart.

Vishnu was looking for a reaction by Sahrindri. But Sahrindri was lost in her thoughts. When she found Vishnu looking at him, she realised she needs to react. "As I said… some people are too innocent to survive in this cruel world," she repeated her words. "And you are the one," she added with a normal smile on her face. "But this is not what you were thinking?" Vishnu contemplated.

"Yes that was not so," Sahrindri accepted after a while. She was so lost in her thoughts that her replies were coming late in a continuous conversation. "Then what are you thinking," Vishnu asked. Sahrindri's eyes weren't on Vishnu, while she was thinking. After a noticeable pause she said, "I am trying to find a link between Indragadh and Dwarka. I am wondering how Agastya is so aware of gemstones if he belongs from a far distant place. Why did he come here?" Sahrindri although murmured to herself, but Vishnu heard all of that?

"What kind of gemstones? What are you talking about? I do not understand." Vishnu put up questions. Looking at him, Sahrindri again murmured, "You need not to know yet." "But why?" when Vishnu asked so, once Sahrindri was paralyzed. She couldn't make it out, what was she going tell him. Aarunya had told her about gemstones, but still that was a secretive story, which couldn't be revealed, unless she had a selfish motive.

"Before knowing about gemstones, hear my story," she said. Vishnu nodded his head to give her consent. Sahrindri started revealing her story. "I belonged from a small village called barista. I was fifteen when one brahmin guy approached me. He fancied me, as I was pretty than other lower caste girls. Else in low born like us, girls aren't really that much pretty. I fell in love with him. He used me emotionally and physically. I had given my everything to him. Then when he was twenty, he married another brahmin girl. I dreamt of marrying him one day. I asked him to marry me, he denied saying that he will never marry a low born like me. Then my parents persuaded me to marry a man of my caste, one who was fifteen years older than me. No matters if he loves me, he is still fifteen years older than me. Life and my parents didn't play nice with me."

After listening to her, Vishnu said, "I am sorry that happened to you." While hearing her, he forgot about gemstones. He felt pity for Sahrindri. "Being betrayed in love is the most devastating thing in the world," said Sahrindri. "I can understand that," Vishnu tried to console her. "No, you cannot… unless you have felt the same thing in your life," Sahrindri argued. "I have faced the same thing. When I came in Indragadh first time, I too had fallen in love with a girl, but she cheated on me. She had relations with one more guy, and she always lied to me," Vishnu's eyes almost watered.

Sahrindri could read his face that he had now revealed the most pathetic part of his life. "Maybe this is why you like my honesty," Sahrindri again tried to hit on him. Vishnu didn't say anything. He was sitting very close to Sahrindri. When two of them shared their part of stories, they connected emotionally with each other. Nobody spoke anything for about half a minute. Then after a while, Sahrindri tilted her face toward him. With hands and legs tied, she made a position to kiss him.

"What are you doing?" Vishnu cried and backed off. "Tell me honestly, whether you have ever kissed that girl or not," Sahrindri asked. "No… I respected her. I did not want to do anything before marrying her," said Vishnu. When he said so, Sahrindri burst in laughter and said, "*To kiss someone, you need lips…not bond of marriage*," Sahrindri said to again mock him. Vishnu gave furious looks at her.

"Now will you tell me…. what you were saying about lord Agastya and gemstones?" Vishnu asked. But certainly, Sahrindri was not the one who could reveal that easily. "I will tell you only after you kiss me," she said and winked. Vishnu was too innocent to ignore such offer by a pretty girl. Vishnu left the room and she kept on laughing at him.

"Hey I am hungry! Bring me some food," she ordered when he went out of the room. "I am not your 24*7 servant," said Vishnu in an exasperating voice. "But you are my keeper. You need to take care of me. Bring me something to eat," she said. "…I am really hungry," she added when she found Vishnu glaring at her persistently. Poor lad had to obey her orders, not just because Agastya had asked him to take care of her but also because his humanity couldn't deny taking care of a prisoner.

While eating, Sahrindri said, "You know what…?" "What?" "I am just wondering why your lord Agastya didn't kill me yet." Sahrindri's wonder was right as according to her knowledge, she was of no use for Agastya. Still, Agastya had prisoned her and not killed her. This bothered her in her thoughts. "Lord Agastya is too kind and soft-hearted to kill anyone," said Vishnu. "I barely had three-four meetings with your lord Agastya, and you know him since your childhood… still, it seems I know him far better than you." Vishnu didn't say anything in response, he was loyal towards Agastya, he couldn't bear hearing wrong words for him. For then, he left the room.

"I am happy that your lord Agastya wants me alive," said Sahrindri after a while. "Why would he want you? He is just kind to not kill anyone," Vishnu mentioned as per his loyalty. But Sahrindri was crafty to figure it out that Agastya wants her alive for some personal benefit.

11

Mystery of Vichitra

Twenty-five years ago, in the realm of Krishnapur.

Prince Mahendra was roaming with his mates near the Sarita river. He was roaming in the forest for the pleasure of his soul. He was enjoying the beauty of nature on the bank of the river. Sarita river was comprehensively flowing over the glistening rocks. A cool breeze was soothing royal face of prince Mahendra. Around the exotic hills and green plants, he was enjoying being a part of nature. The giant hill, milk-white flowing river, lush green plants and the royal prince in between all of them, was a perfect combination. He had his best mates with him and four king's guard to watch over them. Prince was unmarried and according to the fourteenth century was of marriage age. So, as per attribute of his age, he wasn't welcoming the presence of the king's guard there. He wanted isolation in nature with his friends. But being a part of the royal family, he couldn't really roam around the forests without protection.

"These days' father is talking a lot to me about marriage. What you guys think about marriage?" asked prince Mahendra all of a sudden to his mates. Three friends were roaming with him there. They didn't react on his sudden bizarre question. After a while, one of them said, "Are you done sleeping with whores or what?" Prince Mahendra looked frantically at him on his reply. "I don't sleep with whores," he said with confidence in his voice.

"Prince of great empire Krishnapur don't sleep with whores… are you kidding with yourself or with us," said his another mate to mock him and his statement. "I am not lying, and I think I don't have to give proof to anyone about it," said Prince Mahendra. "So you wanna say that you are virgin," said the first mate, who had talked of whores in the first place. He talked of virginity in the way of sarcasm. "Yes I am," said king Mahendra again with confidence in his voice. "So how do you survive without sex in this age," said the third mate. "Need of love should always be more than the need of lust in life," with those words of him he shut their mouth. While talking, they were roaming in the forest.

Three of them didn't speak for a second. When one of them collected words, he said, "So it means for sex you are waiting for love to come in life." "Absolutely," king Mahendra accepted with pride. "And how and when love is gonna come in a prince's life," asked his mate. He emphasised on his words… 'in a prince's life'. Prince Mahendra noticed his prominence. He asked, "Why you think it's hard to come in a prince's life?" "Because commoners like us find love in life by seeing which other commoner is interested in us. But in your case every girl would be interested in a prince like you, then how are going to decide who is the true love of your life," said one of his mate. Another added, "Your marriage is meant to be fixed in another realm's princess by your parents."

Prince Mahendra's friends were disheartening him on the point that he could ever find the true love in his life. But prince Mahendra was persistent on the idea of love. He argued, "Why you all are saying so. Who knows? I may find the love of my life here in this dense forest. Here no one knows that I am the prince of Krishnapur." after saying so he took off his coronet and placed on the head of one of his friend.

King's guards were listening to all of their conversations. Prince Mahendra looked at them disapprovingly. Now he wanted to roam alone with his friends in the forest. "You may leave us for a while now, we'll return to this exact spot," said Prince Mahendra looking at the king's guards. "But my lord, it's not safe for you to be alone with just these boys," said one of them. "We all are grown up enough to take care of ourselves," prince argued. "But my lord, it's king Dharmendra's order to take care of you while you...," Mahendra cut him short, "You are taking care of me while being here. We'll return here in an hour or so," prince Mahendra ordered which king's guards couldn't deny.

Mahendra went in the deep forest with his friends. He wasn't wearing his coronet. One of his friends was wearing the same. "So prince is on love hunt today," one of his friends tried to tease him. Mahendra ignored him. Though definitely, he was a seeker of true love in his life, for then he was just roaming in the forest for inner peace. One must get tired, sitting in a royal palace for too long. He was reliving his stress out. "I am in peace hunt today," he said after a while. They strayed in the forest for quite a reasonable time. All the time prince Mahendra was teased by his friends for searching love in the deep forests.

While they were roaming, they came across a group of beautiful girls. They were tribal girls. "So where this bunch of beauty is heading," said one of prince's mate to tease those girls. "To fetch water," said one of them. She seemed the leader of that group. They had pots with them in their hands. Looking at their royal attires and princely coronet on one of them, they couldn't give a comeback to their tease. There were five girls in that group. All were wearing different colours clothes. All were pretty on their own, but prince Mahendra's eyes stopped on the one wearing white colour attires. She had awestruck looks, and with her perfectly shaped body, she enthralled prince Mahendra's eyes. Prince couldn't take off his eyes from her.

Prince's one mate was wearing the coronet, looking at the girls, he said: "We can have some good time talking here." "It would be our great pleasure to talk with the prince and his friends," said the same girl, who spoke at first. "He is not the prince," said the girl who was wearing white attire. Prince Mahendra was traumatized on her statement. She dazzled him more when she figured it out in just a look that he is not the right prince.

The leader of the group yelled at the girl who was wearing white clothes. "How dare you say so? Can't you see the royal coronet. Apologise to the prince." The girl wearing white clothes didn't apologise in another second. Instead of apologising she added, "the coronet does not really match with the charm he has on his face." When she said so, all other girls got infuriated at her. She had already won prince Mahendra's eyes from her stunning looks, and gradually she was winning his mind and heart, with her audacity and ingenuity. Prince Mahendra's mates remained silent. The one who was wearing the coronet too remained silent, he didn't dare to pretend himself as a prince in the presence of the real prince.

"Your Highness! I apologise to you on her behalf. She is new in our tribe, she doesn't know you…," while the leader of the group was apologising, prince Mahendra came forward and asked, "So, what you think, who is real prince among us?" while asking so, prince was looking in the eyes of girl who was wearing white clothes. She instantly replied, "The one who dared to ask such a question." Lips of prince Mahendra curved right away.

Then prince Mahendra took off the coronet from his mate's head and then he wore the same. When he did so, he made clear to the rest of girls that the girl in white was right in her perception. "May I know the clever girl's name," the prince asked. "Vichitra," she replied. When she told her name, prince's eyes were stuck on her dazzling lips, which had colour as of lotus' petals. "May I have a moment alone with the pretty girl," said Prince Mahendra. She looked towards her mates. That was an awkward moment for all.

After a while prince Mahendra added, "Will you mind if we move alone for a while." He offered to have some quality time alone with the girl who possessed beauty with brain. Prince's mates understood what the prince wanted. One of them said, "Will you girls mind if we leave her and prince in peace." Tribal girls had to agree with them. Then the four girls and three mates of prince Mahendra went and left Vichitra and prince Mahendra alone.

Then there came an awkward silence between them. However, in that silence, prince Mahendra was busy in analysing the beauty of Vichitra. From her pretty face, Mahendra's eyes rolled first on her beautiful neck. Then his eyes rolled down further and found a halt on her beautiful, fair and bare waist. Vichitra noticed him looking at her waist. "I didn't know, you wanted isolation to stare at me or my waist." She was bold enough to dare such words to the prince of the realm. Prince got attention and felt embarrassed.

He then shifted his eyes to her face and said, "No, I wanted to talk to you. I wanted to know you better." Vichitra smiled in response. And once again silence captured in the environment. For absolute five-six seconds, no-one spoke anything. Both of their eyes were looking down, and they were moving together without any destination.

To end the silence, prince Mahendra asked, "So you are new in the tribe. Where were you before coming in this tribe?" Though Mahendra had asked casually, Vichitra remained silent for a coming couple of seconds. It seemed that Mahendra had asked the wrong question at the wrong time. Realising so, Mahendra said, "Have I bothered you." "No… not at all," she swiftly replied. Mahendra remained silent, perhaps he wanted to know, from where she belonged. "I have lived all my life in the forests of Gwalior. I joined this group of the tribe after the sudden death of my parents," she replied at last. "I am sorry that happened to you," said Mahendra. She then exchanged a warm smile with him.

Then they started talking casually, about each other's likes and dislikes. Mahendra was enjoying her company, and so was she. But they were disturbed when Mahendra heard a voice from behind. "Prince shouldn't roam with tribal girls." Mahendra looked behind, and he found Agastya was standing there. Agastya's ponytail was tied.

"Agastya… what are you doing here? Keeping an eye on me," said Prince Mahendra. "No I was just passing by and then just saw you with this girl. You are perhaps forgetting the dignity of being a prince of the realm of Krishnapur," said Agastya in one breathe. "I'll just come," said Prince Mahendra and whispered in Vichitra's ears…, "I'll wait for you in the noon at this same place." Then he went near Agastya and said, "come… we'll move together towards the palace." In his mind,

Mahendra was whispering why did Agastya had to poke his nose in Mahendra's affairs. For then Mahendra left for the palace. He was wondering whether or not the girl in white will come in noon tomorrow.

Mahendra spent the night twisting in his bed. He was lost in thoughts of Vichitra. His friends teased him a lot in the theory of love. Even he hadn't any idea that he would find an attractive girl in the woods. He wanted the morning to come as soon as possible so that he could meet the girl. He spent the night, half asleep. Morning came on its own pace, it didn't hurry for Mahendra.

Mahendra left for the forests soon. He was accompanied by the king's guards. While he was leaving Agastya noticed him. He gave tough looks. It seemed he wasn't really happy with Mahendra seeing the tribal girl. Mahendra being a prince, ignored his looks and left. He soon reached to the spot where yesterday he had whispered in Vichitra's ears that he'll wait for her. Sun wasn't shinning at its peak. Perfect noon still had some time left. Mahendra reached before time.

He didn't find Vichitra just after reaching. It was expected, as he had reached before time. He ought to wait for her. He couldn't even roam around the forest, as he was supposed to not to leave the spot where he had asked Vichitra to come. He waited for around an hour there. He started asking questions to himself that whether or not she'll come. A several time he replied to himself that obviously, she'll come, a he is the prince of the estate and a several time he raised doubt in front of himself that whether or not being a prince is enough to impress a beautiful girl.

His wait ended up with a happy ending. He saw Vichitra coming towards him. He couldn't hide the smile which came on his face when he saw Vichitra. "Pretty lady made me wait for quite a long time," he said when Vichitra came close enough. With a killing smile on her beautiful face, she replied, "No... I didn't make you wait. It seems you came earlier." Mahendra first gazed her entire body. He fancied her a lot. Then after a second, he said, "Maybe, I was more eager than you to meet." Vichitra smiled in response.

"Come let's walk," said Vichitra. Then while walking deep in the forest, they started having simple talks. Both were enjoying each other's company. Vichitra fascinated Mahendra a lot. When the normal conversation came to an end, there came an awkward silence between them. Mahendra was barefacedly staring her impeccably beautiful body. Vichitra's eyes were looking down in that silence. "You are embarrassing me," said Vichitra with a blushing smile on her face. They spent hours talking and starring each other.

"Marry me!" he said all of a sudden to her. Vichitra looked at him with wonder. That was really unexpected from him. She didn't reply for another three-four seconds. "Have I bothered you," he asked, when he got no reply from her side. "There are certain things you need to know about me, before this proposal," she said. "What are they?" "I'll tell you... but not today." "I can wait for you for an eternity," said Mahendra looking in her eyes. "I admire the respect which you are giving to me, but today I will have to leave."

Vichitra then got up to leave. "Will we meet tomorrow," Mahendra asked. "Don't know," she replied. "But tell me where do you live. How will I search for you," Mahendra further asked? As he wanted to make sure that he'll be able to find her whenever he wanted to meet her. "Trust me, we'll meet soon," she said. Mahendra smiled and said, "Then we'll meet right here tomorrow afternoon." Mahendra left after saying so.

In the night when Mahendra was again twisting on his bed. He had spent a few couple of hours with Vichitra, her thoughts were becoming an obstacle in his sleep. While he was trying to sleep peacefully, he suddenly heard someone call him with the use of word 'prince'. Mahendra was sleeping alone in his room, and all the doors of the room were locked by him. He was sleeping in peace. He ignored the voice, he thought that he might have just imagined someone calling him. He was sleeping in his luxurious big royal room. He was sleeping with a turn on his right.

He had ignored the voice at first, he again heard same voice calling him, 'prince'. It was a lady's voice. The second time he was quite sure that somebody is calling him. He instantly got up, when he heard the voice for the second time. His jaw dropped when he got up. He found it was Vichitra who was calling him. She was standing in front of his bed. Mahendra gawked at her with utmost surprise. He couldn't understand how she entered inside the room when he had locked the room. His shock was on peak. Even though he liked her, he couldn't adore her shocking arrival in his room. Her entry could be shocking even in the palace's gate, and she had entered inside his locked room. He wondered how this magic happened, have the guards left the duty, or they slept only for her sudden arrival. He flung the bedsheet and went near her.

"How did you come here?" he asked the obvious question as his first dialogue of conversation with her. "Does that matter at this moment?" She replied. She was smilingly looking at him. She didn't seem a bit tense when she was ought to give explanations of her sudden presence in the locked room of Mahendra. Mahendra was standing next to her. "Vichitra, the room is locked. How did you enter the palace and then in the room?" Mahendra fired questions on her.

She went closer to him. Her boobs touched his bare chest. Then she glided her hand on his chest, and the repeated her word. "Does that matter at this moment?" Mahendra shivered when he felt her touch on his bare upper body. The touch of her boobs had already quivered him, and then a touch of her hand made him melt. For once he forgot on those questions that why and how she entered the palace and in his room. He was feeling her breaths next to him.

"What you mean?" Mahendra asked softly. By now he had forgotten all questions. That was her one touch which made him so. Now instead of again asking how she was there, he asked what she meant by her frisky words. When Mahendra asked what she meant, she again glided her hand on his bare chest and looking in his eyes she said, "Don't you know?"

Mahendra couldn't take off his eyes from her lips. They were perfectly shaped and coloured by god. Looking at her lips, Mahendra whispered, "No." he wanted to hear more playful and naughty words from her. By now he had forgotten about the questions on her presence in the room. He enjoyed the way she seduced him. When she heard the word 'no' from him, she understood that he was enjoying the way she was seducing him. She then again moved her hand on his bare chest and then stopped it on his nipple. She played for a second with his nipple. She didn't say anything.

For next five seconds she kept moving her hand on his chest. Mahendra was standing still and breathing heavily. He couldn't r move or even touch her. With a heavy voice he said, "Why you came here Vichitra, that too in midnight." His question too had changed from how she came there to why she came there. The change of question itself reflected that instead of bothering how she entered, he was enjoying her seduction.

She too understood that he was enjoying her. She gave a killing smile to him and then said, "I came here to make love with my love." She made her purpose clear in front of him. She was still gliding her hand on his bare chest, and he was still looking at her lips. "You are trying to seduce me," said Mahendra after a while. She smiled and then said, "Seduction is an art which requires both heart and brain." Mahendra smiled with naughtiness. Vichitra then pulled him towards the bed. She then bounced on him. He finally placed his lips on hers. Passionately they kissed each other. That night became blissful for both of them. They ripped off each other's clothes and made passionate love. Mahendra was no longer virgin then.

When they were satisfied physically, both of them relaxed. "Now tell me, how you came here?" Mahendra asked her looking in her eyes. She was lying naked next to him. He too was lying naked near her. "So after making passionate love, you want to ask this?" She teased him with her big beautiful eyes. He smiled and floated his hand on her soft cheeks. He then said, "I love you." "So do I" She too replied warmly. He then went closer and kissed her to get ready for round two.

Then in the morning when Mahendra got up, he found Vichitra was gone. He jumped off to check on the door. The door was still locked from inside. Mahendra was shocked with fear. He had ignored how she came inside the room last night. But in the morning she had disappeared from a locked room. His heart was in his hand. He started wondering whether he had sex with a magical or dark magic creature. His body trembled in fear and shock and so did his heart.

He found a note in his room, which was left by Vichitra for him. She had written that she'll wait for him in the noon on the same spot where they had met for the first time. Prince Mahendra had sex with a mystical girl, and now she was asking him to meet her in the forests. In the night time when he was seduced by a beautiful young girl, he had ignored that she entered in room mystically but now when he found her gone from the room, without even opening the locked door, his heart came in his hand in fear. The lady with whom he had sex last night was appearing to be supernatural. Thus fear was valid in his eyes.

He was wondering whether he wanted to meet her alone or not. He was in such a position where he couldn't share anything with anyone. Anxiety was visible on his tensed face. Morning passed by, and unlike yesterday he wasn't ready yet to meet her. Neither his heart was dancing in excitement to meet her. But still, he made his mind to go and see her. He wanted to know about her enigma.

Yesterday he had gone without informing the king, so that he couldn't send kings guards with him. But today he wanted to take kings guards with him. If he asked them to accompany him in the forests, that would be his great humiliation to himself. He wanted to remain bold in his eyes. But the fact remained that he feared to go and meet her alone. He tricked himself, he informed his father that he is going in woods and his father himself did send king's guards with him.

When he reached to the spot where Vichitra asked him to come, he found she was already waiting for him. "It seems someone isn't eager to meet today," Vichitra incepted the conversation. Her eyes were saying that she might be mocking him and his fear. "I am more eager today," Mahendra replied looking at her. Today his eyes were looking in her eyes, instead of lips. "Then why someone is late today and that too accompanied by king's guards." She was absolutely mocking on him and on his fear.

"Father had sent them," he said after a while. Vichitra smiled in response. Mahendra felt as if even her smile was mocking him. "Is the prince of Krishnapur afraid to meet me alone?" she asked. At last, she admitted in words that she was mocking him.

Mahendra asked guards to leave them in peace. He was after all a valiant prince of an eminent empire; how could he depict himself as a coward in front of a pretty lady. When they were alone, Vichitra didn't say anything. She was smilingly looking at him. Looking in her eyes, Mahendra asked, "Who are you?" His question meant whether she was a witch who could appear and disappear in different places.

When he fired that question, she was standing at a distance from him. When he asked so, she went near him and glided her hand again on his chest. She then said, "Do you doubt my love?" "You cannot seduce me today, answer me who are you?" This time Mahendra had princely order in his tone. "I will answer you. If I had any intentions to not to tell you then I would have never come to your room last night," she explained.

"Then answer me, who are you?" prince Mahendra firmly asked. "I am a Nagkanya. I can turn into a snake, whenever I wish too. This is how I entered your room last night." She answered his question the very next moment. Prince Mahendra had heard of Nagkanyas before in his fairy tales, but he hadn't any idea in his scariest dreams whether they existed in real.

"Then what you want from me?" Mahendra asked. If a Nagkanya had approached him that way, shared her secret with him, then definitely she would be in need of some favour from him. She looked in his eyes and said, "I agree that I have entered in your room with a selfish purpose but during our lovemaking, I fell in love with you." Mahendra replied, "Even I have." Mahendra had fallen in love with her, in just one look and lovemaking have augmented that love. The fact of her being a Nagkanya didn't change his feelings for her.

"But still you had taken a risk?" said Mahendra. Vichitra changed her facial expressions to ask, why so? Mahendra continued, "If any of the guards or servants had seen you as a snake, they might have killed you." Vichitra laughed on his statement. Mahendra asked, "What was so funny in that." "I am not just a snake. I am a Nagkanya, I can take care of myself," she replied. "I wonder, how?" Mahendra asked with curiosity. His curiosity stands valid, as when seen, snakes are generally killed by humans.

Vichitra after a pause replied, "We nags live a life according to our wish. We do not age. After reaching young age, we remain young forever. Neither anyone can kill us. We can only be killed by people of our community… with a special dagger, made of snake's skin and teeth." "That's not even heard by us in our stories. So how did your parents die?" Mahendra asked. "I have killed them. They asked me to do so, as they already had lived a hundred and fifty years of life." She replied. "Do nags like you have any disadvantages or just boons in life." Mahendra asked. As benefits told by Vichitra were of a supernatural human, thus, it was quite obvious to ask such questions.

Vichitra's face turned pale when she heard so. It seemed there are a lot of disadvantages in being a nag. "All our life, we need to live hiding from the rest of the world. Every day, we need to change into the formation of snake unwillingly, and that change is full of pain," Vichitra replied. "If you want roses in life then better you should be prepared to face thorns too," she added.

"So what is your selfish motive to meet me and come to my room," Mahendra asked after a while. "Gemstones," she answered. "What kind of gemstones?" Mahendra questioned. Listening to this question of Mahendra Vichitra was baffled, as she wondered how come Mahendra do not know about the gemstones. "How is it possible that you do not know about gemstones. King Dharmendra must have told you about them. It's legacy of your family," said Vichitra. Mahendra pondered, how come she knows about something which Mahendra himself didn't know.

"No trust me, my lady, I don't know anything about any gemstones," said Mahendra. "Then king Dharmendra must be working on them alone," Vichitra murmured. "Explain to me in detail," Mahendra demanded. She sighed and started explaining to him about gemstones. "There is a coronet in your palace which contains four colour's gemstones, red, green, blue and yellow. In one of them, your ancestor's soul is trapped and in one mine ancestor's soul is trapped. They are suffering in them since years. We both need to save our ancestors." She explained him in one breath.

Mahendra then fired unlimited questions, who trapped them, why and how they trapped them, etc. Vichitra couldn't answer any one of them. She was just aware of the fact that there are four souls trapped in those four gemstones and they need to be saved by their forthcoming generations. "But why father never told me about them," said Mahendra. "A father always transfers only happiness' legacy to his son," Vichitra replied. Mahendra understood why his father yet hasn't told him about gemstones.

"But how we are gonna save them," Mahendra asked. "Even I have been looking for this answer since long. Before dying, my parents passed on this legacy to me, that I need to work on gemstones. The same legacy is going on in your family." Vichitra replied. "But what about the other two gems, whose family's ancestors' soul is trapped in those gems," Mahendra questioned. "Don't know." Said Vichitra and added, "I was previously aware of only our ancestors. But in process of finding the coronet carrying gemstones, I learned truth about your family and ancestor."

Mahendra and Vichitra both had half knowledge about gemstones. They were just aware of the fact that they need to save their ancestors. Both of them discussed gemstones and their ancestors for a while. Then Mahendra asked, "Do this Nagkanya still wanna marry me?" He had fallen in love with a girl whose goal was the same as his, then why he wouldn't want to marry her. "That I will answer you tomorrow. For now, I need to leave…. But I need a promise from you that you shall not disclose my identity to anyone," she said. "You need not to ask me that," he assured her.

Mahendra too returned to the palace. When he returned, he saw Agastya coming from the backyard of the palace. "What were you doing there? You are a minister at our palace. You are not supposed to roam in our palace." When Agastya heard so, he tried to hide something from him. "What's that in your hand?" Prince Mahendra asked. When Agastya heard so, he tore the pages he had in his hand. Those were the remaining pages from the translated books of gemstones. So it was Agastya who had torn those pages from that translated book.

When Prince Mahendra saw him tearing some pages. He straight away went to the king and made him aware of the matter. Both king Dharmendra and prince Mahendra insulted him a lot in case of roaming around the palace and tearing some books' pages, without knowledge of king.

"I considered you as my mentor. I honoured you with highest position and you betrayed me by misuing realm's assets.," said king Dharmendra. "You don't deserve to be called as a brahmin," prince Mahendra added. When Agastya heard those words about him, Agastya opened his ponytail and said, "Now I am gonna tie this only when I'll seek my revenge from you." Probably that was the taunt he hated the most.

What he had destroyed was something so crucial that Dharmendra could never bear. He and his generations were trying to save ancestors from their never ending pain. After years they found something fruitful and that too was destroyed.

Though, Dharmendra wasn't aware of books by then. But Agastya's actions made him suspect that he might find something valueable in the palace itself.

He straight away ordered death punishment for Agastya. Soon soldiers came and arrested him and locked him in the prison. Next day when Agastya was supposed to be hanged, soldiers found him missing. In anger Dharmendra ordered death penalty for the soldiers who were in charge of taking care of Mahendra. In anger and frustration of saving ancestors, Dharemendra ordered death penalty for innocent soldiers.

Next day Mahendra went to see Vichitra. She was waiting for him on the same spot. He told her about Agastya. "I doubt he too might know about gemstones and that's why he had entered your palace," said Vichitra. "Well, I don't really think so.... Anyway, leave him. What have you thought about our marriage. I think we should unite for the greater good. For saving our ancestors," said Mahendra. Mahendra wasn't in mood of discussing Agastya with Vichitra. He was desparate to marry him. First time he experienced physical pleasure in his life. This made him little impulsive.

Vichitra sighed and said, "We have a love of only four meetings. Do you think our love deserves a knot of marriage?" "Yes," Mahendra promptly replied. "My mother was a Nagkanya, and my father was a brahmin. So my genes already have the power of nags and brahmins. So marrying you won't benefit me. I should marry a Rajput so that my child should have all the powers of awakening the gemstones. For me, awakening gemstones is the utmost priority," she mentioned. Vichitra specified that she is planning to give birth to a child who would have the power of all four communities, namely, nags, brahmins, Rajputs and low born community. She was doing so because that child will be most powerful and would awake the gemstones.

"How you are so sure that your child will be capable enough to awake the gemstones." Mahendra asked. "This is my own conclusion. Moreover, this is a mere try. I will do anything for saving my ancestors. "You were aware of the fact that you could never marry me… yet, you made me fall in love with you," said Mahendra. He was right in his context that if Vichitra was aware that if she is planning to marry a Rajput guy, then she shouldn't have made him fall for her. "I came in the realm of Krishnapur…with a purpose of stealing gemstones, but then you came in life. I too have fallen for you without any intentions. I am not at fault," Vichitra explained. "But then are you even sure that your child will be able to awaken the gemstones," Mahendra asked the same question again. He wanted her to marry him. This is why he was discouraging him to marry a Rajput guy. "I don't know. I am just using my mind to anyhow save ancestors. Our community is divided into four groups and I presume everyone have their own powers. This is why I am doing so. I'll find a guy who'll have blood of Rajputs and low borns." Mahendra liked her compassion towards her ancestors. He also learnt to feel the same.

Mahendra came near her, held her shoulders from his hands and said, "Alright! Today we pledge to give all our lives to save ancestors. We will release the souls from their agony, pain and years of suffering." Mahendra was a compassionate prince, and thus he too decided to give all his life to save ancestors.

Vichitra smiled. Then both of them passionately kissed each other. Love do not find its destiny in every couple. For having sex, even being a prince Mahendra waited for love. Vichitra came in Krishnapur with purpose of stealing gemstones and ended up sharing her secrets with him. By god's grace, they found love in purest form. But their accountabilities towards their ancestors was hurdle in their love.

At present, in Agastya's home

Agastya was gazing his ugly face in the mirror. He had no expressions on his face. He was gliding his hand in between his open hairs. The strange thing was that in those twenty-five years, he hadn't changed a bit. He looked all young. There was no ageing sign of twenty-five years on his face. He was planning for the upcoming battle. He was a nag who was living a brahmin's life.

At present in the palace of Krishnapur,

Aarunya's mother entered her room. She looked all troubled and worried. She was standing near the table. On table, some fruits and a knife were lying. Queen asked," Aarunya I didn't see you at the dinner table tonight. Is everything alright?" "Mother leave me alone," she replied in anger and frustration. "Aarunya why are you misbehaving with me," said queen softly. Aarunya held the knife in her fist, showed towards her mother and yelled, "Mother I said leave me alone!" "Aarunya!" queen screeched her name, when she saw that form of her daughter.

12

Escape

Like a perfect hostage, Sahrindri was living at Agastya's place. Now instead absconding, she was trying to win over Vishnu. When she was done eating lunch, Vishnu again tied her hands and legs. Lying like a helpless creature, she was gazing at Vishnu. She could see in Vishnu's eyes that he didn't like to tie her hands and legs, 24*7. She had to win him, and in order to win him, she needed to amplify the sense of empathy in Vishnu's heart.

"Now will you tell me about gemstones?" Vishnu asked. "How can innocent minds be curious?" asked Sahrindri with a smile on her face. Vishnu gazed at her for a while and said, "Now will you tell me or not?" he again asked her. He was really curious to know about gemstones and their connection with his master Agastya. "Only after you'll kiss me on my lips," said Sahrindri and laughed out loud. Vishnu made faces at her.

After a while, he tried to say, "Gemstone…," Sahrindri cut him short. "Ssh! Someone is coming" Vishnu closed his opened mouth and looked towards the gate. She was right, Agastya came to see her. "So how is my hostage doing?' He said while entering in the room. Sahrindri looked furiously at him. She didn't say anything, she made a continuous eye contact with him. "What are you doing?" Agastya again asked to mock her.

"Living," she replied after a while, with arrogance. Agastya smiled and said, "That's good." "As that's what you want. You want me alive. Right?" She asked. Agastya smiled at her. He gave her a silent consent. He then looked at Vishnu and said, "Take care of her well." Before leaving Agastya turned towards her and said, "By the way, I have made the king of Indragadh ready to attack the realm of Krishnapur. Your princess Aarunya is in danger!" Sahrindri sighed, gave a half smile and said, "As if I care!" Agastya replied, "I knew it, I know very well what kind of selfish bitch you are." Sahrindri made faces and said, "Still a lot better than you. You are an ugly cunning brahmin with hidden devilish motives." "How can you presume that my motives are devilish?" asked Agastya. "You turned a seventeen year' old girl into a witch…. So your motives ought to be devilish." "Well, I am too busy to answer my hostage," said Agastya and left. He needed to prepare for the upcoming war.

Vishnu was sitting on the chair. About half an hour passed, no one among them said anything. Vishnu started dozing. Sahrindri was in a similar state. After a while, Vishnu screamed. Sahrindri opened her eyes. A snake had bitten him on his leg. Sahrindri saw the snake leaving the room. She had seen snake bit on his leg. She was tied from her legs and hands.

She could only crawl at that moment. She struggled hard to crawl and reach near him. At last, she reached near him. Vishnu was screaming in pain. After reaching there, she started sucking the poison from his leg. She did so for half a minute and then she fell down. Vishnu gained senses. When he woke up, he found Sahrindri was unconscious. He instantly got up to call a Vaidya. Sahrindri had sucked the venom from his leg, he was now fine to get up and call a Vaidya.

He called Vaidya without informing Agastya. When Vaidya came, he untied Sahrindri's hands and legs, so that the Vaidya does not doubt. Vaidya gave her required treatment. Vishnu sat beside her. This time he didn't tie her legs and hands. He was waiting for her to gain conscious. Past story of Sahrindri already made Vishnu empathized for her, now when she sucked venom from his body, he developed more feelings for her.

When she awakened, she saw Vishnu looking at her. She smiled and said, “Seems like someone is falling in love with me.” Vishnu didn’t say anything. He kept on looking at her. “Don’t look at me like that,” she said when she found Vishnu wasn’t taking off his eyes from her. “Like What,” he asked. “Like that,” she too repeated. “Are you blushing?” Vishnu asked. On this, she laughed aloud and started looking in Vishnu’s eyes. At last Vishnu blushed and took off his eyes.

After a pause, he said, “Those lips saved me. I want to kiss them.” When Sahrindri heard so, she couldn’t believe her ears. She had won in her mission. She had won over Vishnu. Now she could abscond with him. Joy danced in her heart. “Then what are you waiting for,” she asked. Vishnu looked at her. He then went closer to her. Slowly he placed his lips on hers. She welcomed him. She started sucking his lips. Vishnu placed his one hand on her cheek and one hand on her bare waist. Then while they were kissing, Sahrindri’s hand went to touch his sword. Immediately Vishnu pulled her back.

“I am not that dumb,” he said after releasing her from his arms. Sahrindri smirked at him. Vishnu then again tied her hands and legs. While he was doing so, Sahrindri said, “I have saved your life. Is this the reward you are giving me? Treating me like an animal. I have not even bathed since days.” “Still I have kissed you,” said Vishnu. That wasn’t expected by Sahrindri from him. She was trying to emotionally blackmail him, but she couldn’t succeed.

"Then why did you kiss me," she asked. "Because you promised me that you'll tell me about gemstones only when I will kiss you on your lips. I have fulfilled my part. Now that I have fulfilled my part, you should tell me about gemstones," Vishnu replied. "You aren't that innocent, I guess," she said. "Hmm," Vishnu accepted. "But I liked that about you," said Sahrindri. She still wasn't in the mood to tell Vishnu about gemstones.

"If you consider yourself honest then you should now fulfil your part and tell me about gemstones," said Vishnu. Sahrindri replied, "Seems like someone has got great implications from my company." Vishnu didn't react. Sahrindri kept on looking at him with dramatic expressions and so did Vishnu. She then said, "Okay! then I will tell you about gemstones but only if you'll tell me that, did you enjoy kissing me." "That was my first kiss, of course, I enjoyed that," Vishnu admitted.

Sahrindri gave lusty looks at him and then said, "I can give you a lot more than just a kiss." Vishnu stared her with no expressions on his face. After a second, he said, "Right now, you just tell me about gemstones. We'll think about that later." Sahrindri needed a selfish motive to tell Vishnu everything about gemstones. Now she was getting one. After saving Vishnu's life, she had already won him a little bit. Then he had kissed her too. Now if she tells him about gemstones, then there were fair chances that she would win over him completely.

After a pause, Sahrindri started speaking. "Aarunya had told me about gemstones. Realm of Krishnapur has a coronet for many years, which contains four colours gemstones, red, blue, green and yellow. They are sleeping gemstones." "What you mean by sleeping gemstones?" Vishnu asked. "It is believed that there are four souls trapped in those gemstones and right now they are sleeping, that means their powers aren't utilised. If they were to be awakened they can give endless power, immortality and eternal beauty to the one holding them." Sahrindri spits out complete truth to him. "It's unbelievable," Vishnu murmured.

His astonishment while listening about gemstones was valid, as Sahrindri had said something he hadn't even heard in fairy tales. "I have seen those gemstones with my eyes. They don't seem to be normal gemstones. Trust me, whatever I am saying is the truth about them," said Sahrindri to assure him that whatever she was saying was all true about gemstones. Vishnu didn't say anything for a second.

Sahrindri asked, "Your lord Agastya is aware of gemstones. He never told you about them?" Sahrindri was aware that if he wants to make Vishnu help her in escaping then certainly, she needs to fade the loyalty he has for Agastya. Thus, she did hit the target perfectly. Vishnu didn't say anything. Sahrindri took advantage of the moment. She added, "I thought he treats you like his son." Vishnu gawked her and said, "Do you think you can make me stand against lord Agastya?" Sahrindri instantly replied, "Yes I can, because your lord Agastya is planning to wear them. He first bribed me to make Aarunya a witch, and now he is planning an attack on Krishnapur. What does this all mean?"

Vishnu remained silent for a while. "Wait for a second, have he told you about the attack on Krishnapur." he was still silent. His silent gestured a no that Agastya hasn't told him anything about the war. How could Sahrindri miss to attack his wounds?

"Agastya treats you no more than his twenty-four hour's servant," she murmured. Vishnu got up to leave the room. "More you'll escape the truth, more it will come chasing you," Sahrindri added. Vishnu didn't pay attention and left.

In the night, Vishnu served dinner to Sahrindri. He untied her hands and kept a sharp an eye on her, with a tight grip on his sword. While eating Sahrindri said, "I am still wondering, why does your lord Agastya wants me alive?" Vishnu didn't say anything. He didn't even look at her. "This time you didn't defend your lord Agastya. Seems like someone is changing his opinion about lord Agastya," said Sahrindri. While looking furiously at her, he replied, "you just have five minutes to finish your dinner." He ordered like a boss that he won't entertain rubbish from hostage of Agastya. Sahrindri being Sahrindri laughed on him and continued with her dinner.

When she was done, Vishnu took her plates, kept them in the kitchen and came back. Unlike other nights, he came back in her room after dinner. He then gazed her for a while. "What?" She said, when she found him continuously looking at her. "You were saying something in the daytime," said Vishnu. "What?" "You said, you can give me a lot more than a kiss. I want to see what?" said Vishnu without expressions on his face. He wasn't even blushing. Sahrindri smirked when she heard so.

"Seems like my kiss has worked like a spark," said Sahrindri with lust in her voice. "No, it worked like coal in the dead ashes," Vishnu replied. "Whatever! I am happy that it worked," she said. Vishnu smiled and said, "So…," "So what?" Sahrindri teased him. Vishnu got up and said, "Fine! Good night." He turned to leave the room. "Wait, wait, wait…. I am ready," she screamed from behind. Vishnu turned, looking in her eyes asked, "Ready for what?"

She smiled. Then after a pause lustily replied, "Ready for everything, but how will that be possible with tied hands and legs." She then showed her hands to him. Vishnu still left the room. She yelled, "Hey! What happened. I said yes for everything. What happened?" She kept on screaming. After half a minute he returned in the room. "Changed your mind again?" she murmured. "No I went to check on the gate," he replied. Sahrindri's heart danced in joy. She was succeeding in her mission.

He then came near her and sat on the floor. "Before untying you, I want to…" He paused. "I want to ….," she insisted him to continue. "I want to kiss those lips again." After listening Sahrindri didn't say anything, she just raised her chin to make a kissing position towards him. That was consent to him. He held her face in his hand and then started kissing her. While kissing, he floated his hands all over her body. He kept on kissing her passionately.

"Ummmm… Ummmm…," she tried to say something in between to him. He released her and looked in her eyes with love. "Untie me…... I want to do so many things," she said. Vishnu smiled and started untying her. When he was done with hands, Sahrindri wrapped her arms around him and started kissing him again. Vishnu pulled her back and said, "Wait… Wait… Wait…. Let me untie your legs too." She laughed and stopped. Vishnu then untied her legs. Just after when she was free from all ropes, she started kissing him more passionately. He too reciprocated accordingly. Then they crossed all the limits. Sahrindri gave him every pleasure that she could give. Vishnu had received more than his mere imagination.

When they were done. Vishnu started pulling clothes back on her bare body. "What are you doing?" She asked. "Nothing! Just trying to help you wear them again," he replied softly. He had love in his voice. She smiled. For the first time, she didn't make fun of his innocence. "I can sleep with you without clothes," she said. They were lying on the floor. Her head was on his shoulder. "But….," he tried to say something. Before he could say, Sahrindri laughed at him. Then she started wearing clothes.

When she was done, she again slept on his shoulder. After a moment they were maintaining eye contact with one another. Looking in her eyes, Vishnu said, "Sahrindri, do you wish to wear those gemstones?" They just had made love, and abruptly Vishnu asked such a question about gemstones. That wasn't expected from him. Sahrindri looked at him and asked, "Why such a question?"

Vishnu then got up. He first wore clothes. Then sighed and said, "Everyone who knows about gemstones will definitely want to wear them. Who does not want endless power, immortality, and eternal beauty? Don't you want all these for yourself?" Listening to his question Sahrindri too got up and replied, "When Aarunya first told me about gemstones, I craved to wear them as a necklace. I craved for all, not just one. But then I realised I can never do so."

After a pause, Vishnu said, "I wish to wear them with you. I wish to live an eternal loved life with you." After hearing that Sahrindri went forward and kissed gently on his lips. She then said, "Generations of the realm of Krishnapur have been trying to awaken them, and all have been unsuccessful." After a pause, she continued, "I do not see dreams of those things that I can't achieve. That makes me helpless in my eyes, and I am a queen of the world in my eyes." Vishnu smiled and kissed her for the round two.

When in morning Vishnu opened his eyes, he found Sahrindri looking at him. In last night's lovemaking, he had forgotten that he was taking care of a prisoner and she could have absconded in that situation. With a jerk, he got up and said, "You didn't run." That was the first question which he asked. She smiled and replied, "I do not want to run without you." Vishnu kept on looking at her. She had already won over him halfway by saving his life from the snake bite, then she made passionate love with him and now by not escaping from the place, she had won him all over.

He went near her. Before saying anything, he, first of all, kissed her again with all his love and passion. "Now I won't let you rot here for even a second. I owe my life to you," he said. "You have saved my life from a snake bite. I owe my complete life to you," he repeated. Then expeditiously they ran away from Agastya's secret house. Sahrindri and Vishnu proceeded to move towards Dwarka.

In the evening when Agastya came to take a round. He didn't find them in the room. He smirked and remained silen. It seems like he wanted Sahrindri to escape with Vishnu. His plans were working accordingly. But he didn't had time to celebrate, he had more important tasks to accomplish. He headed towards the palace where king Ashoka was waiting for him. They had a final meeting about the war. As tomorrow was

Saturday, the planned day when they were supposed to attack Krishnapur.

13

Another Sacrifice

"Chitrangna get up. Sun has already risen, and you are still in your bed," said queen Vichitra to her daughter Chitrangna. Chitrangna removed the blanket from her body and got up. "Good morning mother," she said. "You need to get ready. You'll be meeting the king of Krishnapur and the prince today." "But why? I am in no mood of getting married right now," she said. "And how did you presume that we are making you meet them for the purpose of your marriage?" Vichitra asked. "These days, father is making me meet princes of different realms for the purpose of marriage only," she replied. Vichitra sighed. Chitrangna was right, king Vashisth was really worried about the marriage of his young daughter, and he was asking her to meet princes of different kingdoms. Contextually her presumption cannot be stated wrong from any means.

Vichitra didn't say anything. She was busy folding the blanket that Chitrangna had put on. "Mother…" "What?" "When will you tell me how to trigger my nag's side," she said out of the blue. Vichitra dropped blanket from her hands and stared at her and softly murmured, "Ssh! I have told you a hundred times to not to utter about us being Nagkanyas every now and then." "But mother, father will make me marry anytime, and before that I want to become a complete Nagkanya, just like you. Immortal, powerful and eternally beautiful. I wonder why father hasn't doubted you by now," said Chitrangna.

Chitrangna added, "You have already triggered brother Chitrang's nag's side….," Vichitra cut her short. "Thousand times I have warned you to not to talk about your brother."

Vichitra roared at her. Chitrangna kept silent. She might have disturbed her mother by talking of her brother Chitrang.

Vichitra gazed her for a while, she was looking like an innocent child asking her mother for a toy. Then Vichitra went near her and said, "you are my daughter and more than you, I want see you as a complete Nagkanya. But before that, you'll have to accomplish so many important tasks." "Like what?" "You'll know soon." Then Vichitra helped Chitrangna to get ready for a royal meeting.

There in the guest room, Aarav and Mahendra too were getting ready. "Father are you in the mood to tell me what you are going to do? I saw you going out of the room in midnight, but you gave me no explanations about that," said Aarav looking at his father. But king Mahendra wasn't paying attention to him. He was busy putting his ornaments on his bare chest. "Father, answer me." Aarav insisted again. Mahendra looked at him and said, "I am already repenting my decision to bring you here with me. Don't ask anything and bother me." He made Aarav silent.

Then both left the guest room and proceeded towards the main hall where king Vashisth was waiting for them along with his daughter and wife. When they moved there, Aarav tried to notice whether his father and queen of Ratnagadh will share the same smile or not. But this time nothing like that happened.

"So, how is the morning of king and prince of Krishnapur in the realm of Ratnagadh?" asked king Vashisth. "It has been greater than our assumptions," king Mahendra warmly replied. Then they formally hugged each other. King Vashisth offered seats to them. "I am so grateful for you for this friendly visit."

"Trust me, we are more delighted than you," Mahendra replied.

Then after some light conversations, Vashisth said, "How about converting this friendship into a relationship. My daughter has turned nineteen, and your son seems perfect for him." He offered that proposal so abruptly that Mahendra couldn't reply. He hadn't made a friendly visit to Ratnagadh. He had visited because Vashisth's daughter can now probably help them to awaken the gemstones. Thus, he couldn't reply to his sudden proposal instantly.

After a while, he collected words to reply to him. "Oh! Yes, we'll think about that." Aarav gave a look at Chitrangna. He found her attractive enough to marry. Chitrangna on the other side was looking at her mother. She was perhaps saying that look father is again talking about marriage and you need to trigger my nag's side soon. Who on this planet wouldn't want to be immortal and eternally beautiful. Nags had different lives. They could be only killed by someone from their own community, that gave them a sense of immortality, as they do not age either. Power, on the other hand, they possessed more than a normal human being. Thus, the eagerness of Chitrangna for becoming a Nagkanya was obvious. Mahendra's day passed chatting with king Vashisth.

In the night, king Mahendra got up. He found Aarav sleeping tranquilly on his bed. He did not want Aarav to notice him going out. He left the room and again went to the same place where he had met queen Vichitra last night. The Queen was already waiting for him.

"Have you told Chitrangna?" that was the first question Mahendra asked Vichitra. She nodded her head to convey a denial to his question. "Then what are you waiting for? Tomorrow is the night when we'll perform the dark magic on her," said Mahendra. Vichitra sighed and said, "What we are doing is just a trial. Chitrangna has the blood of all four powers in her blood. I have given her power of nags and brahmins, cause my father was brahmin and mother was a Nagkanya. Her father has given her powers of Rajputs and low born people, cause his father was a Rajput and mother was a low born...," "That makes her perfectly eligible to awaken the gemstones. She is the most powerful creature on the planet," Mahendra cut her short. "Still we aren't sure if this will work or not," said Vichitra.

Mahendra held her shoulders, looked in her eyes and said, "Vichitra all that we can do is try our best." "But she'll never agree to kill her own father for the sake of our mere try," she replied. So, basically, Mahendra and Vichitra were converting the most powerful creature of the planet into a witch so that she can awaken the gemstones. That was a mere try for them, they weren't sure whether that would work or not. "Then what you have planned?" asked King Mahendra. That was the only question left in his heart. Vichitra had called him from the realm of Krishnapur to the realm of Ratnagadh just because she felt that now she can help to awaken the gemstones and save their ancestors. Consequently she must be having something in her mind.

"The dark magic will be performed on me," she replied after a while. "What? What will be the benefit of that?" King Mahendra asked in wonder. "I will kill Vashisth because Chitrangna will never do so," she added. "Do you love him?" he asked. His question had emotions. In the past twenty years, he had never stopped loving her. For that particular dark magic, it was necessary to kill someone you love. Thus Mahendra had the curiosity to know whether Vichitra loved her husband or not. Vichitra understood in a second, why he was asking so. Smilingly she replied, "Time is no less than magic. It can even make you fall in love with someone you don't want to."

Mahendra didn't reply anything. He could collect no words to reply. For a few seconds, he didn't speak anything. Then he remembered about gemstones, he said, "But I am sure you won't be able to awaken the gemstones and save ancestors. Chitrangna, on the other hand, can probably do so." Vichitra confidently replied, "Dark magic will be performed on me, but the results will be reaped out by none but Chitrangna." "How is that even possible?" he interrogated.

Mahendra's only target was to awaken the gemstones and save the ancestors. He had travelled so far for the same purpose. He was looking for an answer from Vichitra. She took time of three seconds to reply. "Chitrangna is asking me to trigger her nag's side since years. I will ask her to cut my arm and drink my blood to trigger her nag side. That way dark magic will pass on to her veins from mine."

Mahendra understood what she meant. She had told him that Nagkanyas like her can be killed only from someone like them. Thus, if she'll make Chitrangna kill her, then she'll be sacrificing her life for saving ancestors.

He went near her and looking in her eyes said, "Are you saying to sacrifice yourself." "Yes." "No you cannot do so," said Mahendra with emotions. "There is no other option left Mahendra. Ancestors are suffering since years and its high time we save them. I believe I have lived my life, now it's my duty to save ancestors," she said. Mahendra kept silent for a moment. He had loved Vichitra, right after he had seen her. To save ancestors, they couldn't live together and now to save them she was asking to sacrifice her life. He went closer to her and looked in her eyes with love. "I love you," he said while his eyes were fixed on hers. Mahendra too was determined to save ancestors, that he could not argue with her further and ask her to not to sacrifice herself

"I'll be cheating with my daughter," she said. Mahendra was expecting an I love you too from her side. But what she said was different. "And how is that?" "To trigger her nag's side, she needs to do something else. Drinking my blood will not help her to trigger her nag's side. I'll be fooling her." "Whatever we are doing has a good cause," Mahendra consoled her. She nodded her head.

After a pause, Mahendra asked, "So tell me what I need to do?" He was asking her to guide him about her plan. She replied, "Tonight I will tell Chitrangna about gemstones and ancestors. Then tomorrow we'll perform the dark magic, I'll bring Vashisth to the place. Then after my people will call Chitrangna to the place where we'll be performing dark magic on me. I will make her drink my blood to transfer the magic. Then after my death…." Mahendra cut her short and uttered her name with affection. "Vichitra…" "That'll be a sacrifice to save ancestors. Don't you worry about me. After my death you will take Chitrangna to Krishnapur, to figure it out what to do with gemstones," she recited her plan in one breathe.

Mahendra still could not gulp the fact that Vichitra will be dying coming night. "I will miss you," he said in wheezing voice. "Promise me that you'll not let my sacrifice go waste and you'll be the last king of Krishnapur who'll take the weight of saving ancestors on his shoulders," said Vichitra. Mahendra held her hands in his and said, "I promise you that I'll give my best." "We'll perform the dark magic referred in the books that your father found and I'll use my experience that by giving birth to a child who has powers of all communities, brahmins, nags, Rajputs and low born, we can awaken gemstones," said Vichitra. "Tomorrow just follow the nags from here, and they'll bring you to the right place," she added. Mahendra was in emotions that moment, thus he couldn't say anything. "I am sure, things will work out this time," he said and kissed her. Tomorrow she was going to sacrifice her life. Thus he made his last kiss to her passionately. Then both of them left for their rooms.

Instead of entering her room, Vichitra headed towards Chitrangna's room. She needed to talk with her about gemstones and ancestors. She was awake. "Mother," she uttered when she saw her mother entering her room. "What brings you here at this time," she asked. That was an odd timing when Vichitra had visited her room. "What do you think, what bought me here," she cross-questioned. Chitrangna stared at her for a while. With lust for power in her eyes, Chitrangna replied, "Maybe you are in the mood to trigger my nags side." Vichitra smiled and said, "I want to tell you something else… something more important than triggering your nag's side." "What could be more important than this?" Chitrangna asked.

Vichitra who was standing, went near her bed and seated next to her. Chitrangna was looking for answer to her questions. Vichitra first caressed her hand in between her hairs. "Do you wanna know why the king of Krishnapur made a sudden visit to our palace?" asked Vichitra. She was in the mood to open some knots. Chitrangna nodded her head to say a no in gesures. "He visited because I personally called him," she replied and left Chitrangna in wonder. "What?' Chitrangna cried. "I thought father had called them," she added.

Vichitra sighed and said, "All that your father know is that they had visited for a friendly meeting with us." Chitrangna's facial expressions changed into more of wonder. As she couldn't infer why her mother will call a king from a realm, without knowledge of her father. But she didn't utter anything, she was looking at Vichitra's face with surprise. Her expressions were themselves demanding answers from her.

Vichitra then said, "King of Krishnapur and I have something in common." She was making Chitrangna more baffled. Her mother had something in common with some other king, she couldn't think anything relatable. All that she could do was to wait for her mother to continue. Vichitra continued. "There are four sleeping gemstones in the realm of Krishnapur which if awakened can give immortality and powers beyond imagination." "What?" Chitrangna couldn't stop herself from uttering that word. She too was a young girl, who wanted to remain eternally beautiful by any measures. Thus the fact of immortality definitely attracted her.

"Is that the thing common between you and king of Krishnapur, that you both want to awaken those gemstones," asked Vichitra. Her inferences were mostly indicating that she was badly craving to become a Nagkanya and become powerful, thus everything consisting power was attracting her. Vichitra denied by nodding her head. "Then what's the common thing between you and king of Krishnapur." She inquired.

Vichitra took a pause to reply. "One of my ancestor's and one of King Mahendra's ancestor's soul is trapped in two of those gemstones since years. In all four gemstones, four souls are trapped. Generations of Krishnapur realm have been trying to save those souls but they all failed." "What souls…. Who trapped them inside the gemstones… and why they trapped them?" Chitrangna fired questions. "Even I don't know answers to these questions. I just know that four souls are in great pain since years and we need to save them for the sake of humanity… for the sake, I share blood with one of them," Vichitra replied.

"And how you are going save them?" Chitrangna asked. Vichitra now needed to tell her that Chitrangna herself might be the one to save them, as that was their plan. So now her words needed to be chosen more wisely than before. Vichitra took a longer pause. Chitrangna was silently looking for an answer.

"I am not going to save them, you can save them," she finally said those words. Wonder on Chitrangna's face heightened than before. "What do you mean?" She asked. "You have powers of all four communities with you. I had the powers of Brahmins and Nagkanyas. Your father had powers of Rajputs and low born community, and you are our daughter, which makes you a holder of power of all. I guess that makes you perfectly eligible to awaken the gemstones." Chitrangna didn't say anything. She was listening to everything unusual and weird.

"Tomorrow I'll be asking you to do some acts, that will trigger your nag's side. Promise me that you'll do whatever I say." Vichitra manipulated Chitrangna by saying that she'll be triggering her nag's side, when in fact her motive was just to transfer the dark magic inside her. "I promise, I'll do whatever you say," Chitrangna gave her consent. "Good night then," said Vichitra and left. She had left Chitrangna in flood of questions.

Next night Vichitra awakened Vashisth in the midnight. "What happened Vichitra? What is bothering you at this moment?" he asked when she had troubled his sleep in the middle of the night. "I have some urgent work with you. I need to tell you something," she said. "At this moment. What could be so important?" asked Vashisth. He couldn't gauge what was making his wife ask such inexplicable thing and that too at an awkward moment.

"You need to come with me right now. It's urgent. That's all I can tell you at this moment," she said. She left Vashisth with no other option except to come with her. When they came out of the palace, he asked, "Where are we heading?" "Just follow me." "We should at least take guards with us. Its night time, it won't be safe for a king and queen to wander like this," said Vashisth. He had an alarming tone which asked Vichitra that she must listen to him.

"Trust me we won't need any guards. Just trust me once," she said. "I have trusted you all my life," he replied with confidence. He was in so much love with her that he couldn't deny her for anything. Quietly he followed her. She started moving towards the woods. "Vichitra, in the midnight what sort of urgency do you have in the middle of the forest," he asked. Vichitra was doing such weird things that even so much of love could question. "You just need to trust me for an hour. It is for the greater good," said Vichitra. Poor Vashisth had to inaudibly follow her.

Soon they reached the place where Vichitra had made all the arrangements for the dark magic to be performed. Vashisth saw an old lady sitting on a rock, and in a corner he found Mahendra standing and looking towards him. In a second he couldn't predict what all was happening. His wife took him to the dark forest in the midnight, and king of some other realm was already waiting for him. That old lady was also giving him doubtful thoughts.

"What is happening here?" he yelled, looking at Vichitra. His eyes were questioning her that how come she took him to a place where some other man is already waiting for her. Vichitra held his hand and said, "Come!" Reluctantly, he followed her. She took him near a giant tree. Then she made him stand straight. He was numbed to react anything. He couldn't comprehend what was going on. Soon two soldiers came from the dark forests and tied Vashisth to the tree with the help of a rope. He was too dazed to even yell or defend himself. His beloved wife had tied him to the tree. She had done those things in front of some other king, so certainly she had done those things with the help of him. He could not react. He was numbly looking at Vichitra. Years of love flashbacked in front of him. When he peeped into the past, he asked himself, whether she is the same Vichitra or she is hers' identical twin.

For once Vichitra made eye contact with him. When she found Vashisth's eyes were looking at her, she said, "I am not even sorry!" She bluntly said those words. Vashisth had no idea what her purpose was? A tear rolled down his eyes. Mahendra went near him and said, "I am really sorry for all this. But whatever we are doing is for the greater good." Vashisth gave a look at him. When Mahendra said so, Vichitra said, "Sorry is a word used by those who aren't sure about their actions. Nothing like that ever happened to me."

When Mahendra found Vichitra uttering brutal words in front of Vashisth, he went near her and said, "You should at least once explain king Vashisth why we are doing all this?" If Mahendra wanted, then he too could have given him explanations, but it was Vichitra who had betrayed him. Thus he deserved a little explanation from her. Vichitra gave tough looks at Mahendra. Probably she was saying that she doesn't really think so that she owes an explanation to him. From his facial expressions, Mahendra insisted her to do so.

Vichitra went near Vashisth and said, "In the realm of Krishnapur, there are four souls trapped in four gemstones. We don't know who, how and why trapped them inside those gemstones. All that we know is, mine and King Mahendra's ancestors' souls are trapped in two of those gemstones. They are suffering since years, and we need to release those souls, end their pain. For that process, I married you to give birth to a child who has powers of all communities so that she could help us in saving our ancestors. Now I'll kill you to enter dark magic in my veins.......," Mahendra cut her short, "She is supposed to kill someone she loves. She actually loved you. It's just because of ancestors, we are doing this evil."

The way Mahendra explained Vashisth, said a lot about his empathetic soul and compassionate personality. Vichitra added, "Later on Chitrangna will kill me. Dark magic will pass in her body through me. Else she could have never killed someone she loved. That's all from my side." Vichitra offered a formal explanation to him. Mahendra didn't like her behaviour.

"You could have asked me once what you wanted. I would have given you my life," said Vashisth looking at Vichitra. "Well, that's exactly, what I want," said Vichitra bluntly. Vashisth couldn't gather words to speak. In just one minute, his life not only changed drastically but also had come to an end. He didn't open his mouth to say anything. He kept on looking at Vichitra. Vichitra had mentioned that she'll be taking his life. All that happened in just half a minute. Years of love changed in less than a minute.

Vichitra on the other hand, moved towards the old lady and sat beside her on a rock. She then said, "Start!" Old lady lighted the fire. Then the old lady started chanting dark mantras. She started revolving around the fire. Vichitra was sitting near the fire, and the old lady was roaming around the fire and around her. She was also putting some dark matter into the fire and was chanting the dark mantras.

Mahendra was gazing at her. Soon his love was going to sacrifice her life for the sake of ancestors, his eyes were watering while looking at Vichitra. But his eyes also had relief seeing that after years of trial, gemstones would be awakened and ancestors would be saved. Vashisth, on the other hand, was already dead seeing the love of years vanished in just a minute. All his life had changed in a minute.

For about an hour, the dark magic was performed by the old lady. Today there was no moon night. Sitara night was to lessen the effect of dark magic, but Mahendra had planned to enter dark magic inside Chitrangna with all power so that there remains no lacuna in their try to awaken the sleeping gemstones.

Then the old lady went inside her hut and bought a bowl full of human blood. She handed the bowl to Vichitra. Old lady kept on chanting the dark mantras. Then she ordered Vichitra to drink the human blood. Vichitra then gulped the human blood down her throat in one breathe. The old lady cut Vichitra's hand and poured the blood in the fire. The old lady then chanted few more mantras. Vichitra was already prepared to kill Vashisth, thus after the dark magic entered inside her, the urge to kill her loving husband heightened in her heart. Vashisth died a million times when he was seeing his beloved wife, performing that dark magic. Only a mere formality remained to end his dead life.

The old lady gave her the dagger. She got up from the rock she was sitting on. Vashisth's eyes were on her. He was gazing her constantly, since an hour. It seemed that even if he weren't tied, then too he wouldn't have escaped. He was that much shattered from what she had done to him. With dagger in her hand, Vichitra proceeded near Vashisth. Mahendra too came near him and said, "I am really sorry king Vashisth, all this happened to you." Vashisth didn't even look at him. His eyes were constantly staring at Vichitra, a woman who had no shame in what she was doing. She was so lost in her mission of saving the ancestors.

Her grip on the dagger was firm. "I am glad that in all these years you gave me enough love to love you back. I can accomplish my mission only because I loved you," she said. Vashisth didn't react. After a second's pause, Vashisth asked,

"Are you sorry?" "No!" She replied and ran the dragger on his neck. Blood started splitting out from his neck hastily. Mahendra closed his eyes in grief. In no time living Vashisth turned into a dead body.

"Clear the body, fast!" said Vichitra to the soldiers standing nearby. They untied Vashisth and took the dead body inside the hut of the old lady. Vichitra looked at Mahendra, his face had grief's signs. "If you'll grief such losses this much, then you won't be able to save ancestors. Vashisth had the pain of few minutes and ancestors are suffering since years. Saving them is more important than anything else," she said while looking at king Mahendra. He looked at her. Vichitra added, "I am sacrificing myself and leaving everything on you. I hope you'll not let my sacrifice go waste."

Mahendra who was standing a bit far from her went near her and looking in her eyes said, "I will never let your sacrifice go waste. Call Chitrangna." "She'll be here soon." So, Vichitra had planned to call Chitrangna after killing Vashisth. Helplessness of Vichitra was unexplainable. Years before she had sacrificed the first love of her life for saving the ancestors and accomplishing her duties towards the soul of her ancestors. Then she loved a king for years, whom she murdered for the greater good. Her son had hidden mysterious life. Her daughter was being prepared to be a witch and she is going to sacrifice her life soon.

Soon, Chitrangna came with other two soldiers. When Chitrangna saw Vichitra, she said, "Mother! why you called me in a dark forest in midnight." "To trigger your nag's side… that's what you wanted all your life. Right?" Chitrangna looked at Mahendra, she found it awkward that she talked about nag's side in front of King Mahendra. “Yes, mother,” she replied. Even in the awkward presence of King Mahendra, she couldn’t hide her craving to become a Nagkanya.

“But before that, you need to promise me that you’ll do certain things.” said Vichitra. “What?” she softly asked. “Last night I had told you about gemstones and souls trapped in them.” Chitrangna nodded her to give her consent. “Promise me that after I trigger your nag’s side, soon you’ll help king Mahendra in awakening gemstones,” Vichitra added. “I promise I will,” Chitrangna confirmed that to become a Nagkanya, she would do anything.

“Then do, what I say,” said Vichitra to Chitrangna. “What mother?” she asked. Vichitra took another dagger which had snake’s skin’s imprint on it. Looking at dragger Chitrangna felt petrified. She wasn’t expecting that her mother will ask her to do something like that. But she didn’t say anything. She was waiting for her mother to instruct her, what to do. Mahendra was controlling his emotions. Soon the love of his life will die in front of his eyes, and he couldn’t even cry.

“Cut my hand’s vein from it and start drinking my blood,” said Vichitra looking at Chitrangna. “What?” Chitrangna bawled. She was in trauma even while looking at the dagger, and now her mother had asked her to cut her vein and start her own drinking blood. Even in her scariest nightmare, she wouldn’t have dreamt to do something like that.

“Mom, you are crazy,” she said. “Chitrangna there is no other option. To trigger your nag’s side, you have to do it. You have to cut my vein from this knife and drink my blood until I faint,” said Vichitra. Chitrangna was craving to become a Nagkanya, but still, her craving hadn't gone to that peak where she could kill her own mother.

"Mother I cannot kill you to trigger my nag's side," she said in a wheezy voice. "You will not be killing me. I will just faint once, and after that, I'll resurrect," said Vichitra to console her. Mahendra came near her and said, "Trust your mother, Chitrangna." Chitrangna looked at him to ask who are you to say so. "Chitrangna, this is how I had become a Nagkanya. This is a ritual that every girl from our family needs to perform. Now you have to just hurry up!"

When Vichitra said that she too had performed the same ritual, she saw a sign of approval on Chitrangna's face. "Don't think much Chitrangna, just do it," she again asked her to cut her vein and drink her blood until she faints. "Are you sure, you are going resurrect after this?' She asked. "Yes Chitrangna, just do it!"

Then with trembling hands, she cut her right hand's vein. "Aahh!" Vichitra cried. Both Chitrangna and Mahendra closed their eyes once. Blood started flowing out from her wrist. "Drink Chitrangna, Drink!" Vichitra yelled. "You need to do this to become a Nagkanya!" said Vichitra again. "Don't think of me. I'll get up again. Just drink."

Then Chitrangna started drinking the blood of Vichitra from her hand. She started sucking the blood endlessly. Slowly life started leaving from Vichitra's body. Mahendra died a thousand deaths at that moment. He couldn't stop his tears. While Chitrangna was drinking blood from her hand, Vichitra's eyes were continually looking Mahendra. Both of them were saying a silent 'I love you' to each other.'

In no time Vichitra fainted on the ground. Chitrangna left her and cried, "Mother!" Looking at her, Vichitra said, "Promise me that you'll help king Mahendra in saving the ancestors." "Mother why are you saying so. It seems like these are your last words! Won't you resurrect?" Asked Chitrangna with tears in her eyes. Vichitra then closed her pretty eyes for forever.

14

The Attack on Krishnapur

It was Saturday morning. There was a lot of disturbance in the palace of Indragadh. They were supposed to attack the realm of Krishnapur. Agastya hadn't had enough sleep last night, and same was with king Ashoka. King Ashoka was sleepless, thinking of Aarunya. He wanted to win at any cost. Agastya, on the other hand, was however sure about the victory but more than the war, he was concerned about the gemstones. He had to plan to grab the gemstones under his possession, after his victory.

Chief of the army of the realm of Indragadh had arranged the army by climbing on the hill. There was one hill which segregated the realm of Krishnapur and the realm of Indragadh. The army was supposed to be arranged accordingly. Planning was done, from where they'll climb and how they'll reach down. As per Agastya's decision the first two lines was set of archers, followed by the army of swordsman. Realm of Indragadh had the advantage of more number of men with them. By placing their weak men on the front, they had reaped benefits of their advantages very well. The army was ready to move on towards the hill.

King Ashoka wore his armour and sat on his chariot. He looked towards Agastya, he too was ready on his chariot. Ashoka ordered chariot rider to take the chariot near him. Then after reaching near him, Ashoka said, "Agastya, I want you to reconsider your presence to the battle." It was early morning, the troop was ready to leave the battle, and Ashoka was asking Agastya to reconsider his decision of coming in the battlefield. He gave a look to Ashoka.

After a pause, Agastya said, "Your Highness! Trust me you would need me in the battlefield." Though Agastya wanted to say that you cannot win the war without me, but he changed his words and molded them in rather a modest way. "I don't want to lose you," said Ashoka. "I will take care of myself. You barely know me. I am quite good in the battlefield. You just know me for three years. There are lots of things that you need to understand about me," Agastya tried to convince him that he could handle the war.

But Ashoka wasn't convinced. He wanted to make sure that Agastya should be with him always as his mentor. "But...," Ashoka opened his mouth to say something. But Agastya cut him short. "Right now your concern shouldn't be me. Your only concern should be the war. We need to win it," said Agastya, he kind of proclaimed that he is firm on his decision of joining the war and he is not going to change it. Ashoka couldn't say anything else.

Agastya then gave a look to the army. Those were the men who will fight for his personal purpose. He smiled cunningly while looking at the army. Agastya had planned a sudden attack on Krishnapur, and the realm of Krishnapur had less than fifty thousand people in their army. Moreover, the number of cavalry was also greater in number in the realm of Indragadh. On the other hand, Indragadh had seventy thousand men in their force. Only their archers were weak, but the other points were indicating that Indragadh was at an advantage.

While Agastya and Ashoka were busy staring at their men, chief of the army came near them on his horse. He halted his horse and pulled the straps. Both Ashoka and Agastya's eyes were on him, they understood, he had come to say something significant. "Your Highness!" he greeted the king.

"I will insist you once again to reconsider your decision of placing our archers in the first two lines. I am scared that it will give negative results." Said the chief of the army. He desired to save all and Agastya just desired to win the war. "We have already discussed the matter, and I am still with Agastya's decision. The formation is perfect to lead a war on a hill with the best swordsman." Said Ashoka. Chief of the army couldn't argue further.

The cavalry then charged to the hill. They started moving up. First two line of archers made the first move on the hill, followed by the swordsman. Like any other war formation, the king was protected well by the soldiers. King Ashoka ordered to give the same protection to Agastya. Agastya willingly rode his chariot close to the chief of the army. He was nearest to the chief of the army. he could even talk to him in the middle of the battlefield.

Soon, the heavy troop was visible to the few soldiers of Krishnapur, who were sitting on the border of Krishnapur and Indragadh. Looking at the heavy troop, they understood in another moment that it's an attack on the realm of Krishnapur by the realm of Indragadh. They ran towards the palace to alarm the queen and princess about the war. Though it was an unalarmed attack by looking at the march of the heavy troop, but looking at the number of soldiers marching towards Krishnapur, anyone could say that it was an attack. The soldiers who were sitting on the hill, ran towards the palace.

The two three soldiers entered the palace shouting, 'Attack! Attack! It's an attack on us by Indragadh." Aarunya was sitting alone in her room when she heard so. In the absence of her father and brother, she was in charge of Krishnapur. 'How could they attack us… they are our friends.' That was the first thought which knocked her mind when she first heard the word 'attack.' But that wasn't the correct time to make an analysis about why they attacked. The important thing that moment was that they attacked and they needed to defend themselves against them.

Her legs made her first run out of the room, to her mother. But then she remembered something and she turned her legs back towards her room. She re-entered her room and moved towards the cupboard. Her eyes got fixed on the coronet. She remembered the old lady's prophecy, who said that a realm will attack your estate and you are going to need powers to protect your gemstones. Her soul trembled remembering her words. It seemed like she has entered a dark tunnel and she cannot spot light in the tunnel.

She then remembered more of her words. The old lady had also made a prophecy that in order to protect her gemstones, she would need to kill someone she loves. To complete the ritual, she was asked to kill someone she loves. She was already getting the urges to kill her mother, and now destiny has given her the motive too. She was expected to save her realm from the attack of another estate. Moreover, all the prophecies of that old lady were coming true, so consequently as per predictions of that old lady, her gemstones were in danger and in order to protect them, she would kill someone she loves. Aarunya might be hungry of power, immortality ans eternal beauty but her souls wasn't shameless enough to kill her own mother.

While Aarunya was lost in her thoughts, her mother entered her room. She had been controlling her urges for many days. "Aarunya, it's an attack on our realm. Indragadh has attacked us," said her mother in quivering voice. "You should have not come in my room at this moment," she said while looking at her mother. Her eyes were red. Devil that inside her, during the dark magic was begging to come out. Her mother couldn't understand what she meant. She had entered her room to alarm her about the war, and in turn, Aarunya reacted weird.

Queen moved near her and yelled, "Aarunya, it's an attack on our realm, send a message to your father fast else....," queen couldn't complete her sentence. "Mother please go away," she yelled. Her eyes watered in excessive aggreassion. Queen couldn't forsee what was happening with her daughter "Aarunya, what happened? Don't panic this much, else how we'll protect our realm. Inform your father soon."

"Mother!!!!!!!" This time Aarunya bawled at her peak. She then held the knife placed in fruit's basket. "Aarunya!" Queen cried when she saw her daughter in that state. She was fighting with herself, to not to kill the queen. "I am so so so so sorry," said Aarunya while crying. "Sorry for what?" Queen still cannot predict that she had grabbed the dagger, to kill her. All that she could think was that Aarunya is baffled due to sudden attack.

Aarunya was failing to control her urges. Her devil was winning against her humanity, emotions and everything positive. She headed towards her mother while holding the knife. Like every normal mother, queen still couldn't predict that her beloved daughter is preparing herself to kill her. "I am gonna kill you," Aarunya cried with wheezing voice and watering eyes.

"Aarunya what rubbish you are talking during this emergency. I am your moth…." She couldn't complete her thought, Aarunya entered the dagger inside her stomach. "Aahhh…!! She cried in pain. A dagger in stomach wouldn't kill you in seconds. She was moving towards deaath with the thought that her own daughter had killed her. Not even in hers scariest nightmare, she had presumed so. With tears in her eyes, she said, "Aarunya!"

Aarunya begain crying loudly. She was seeing her mother moving towards death and the reason was Aarunya herself. "Mother I was helpless. Sahrindri fraudalently performed dark magic on me." Aarunya tried to explain her." "Gemstones," this was the last word of queen before she died. Aarunya cried her heart out. Queen dies saying that Aarunya's greed had killed her mother. Aarunya couldn't cry for the moment. As her realm and specially her gemstones were in danger.

After a while she came out, her mother's body wasn't visible anymore. She proceeded to meet her realm's chief of the army. Her feet were hurrying up. Realm of Krishnapur have faced an attack, and she was in charge at that time. Most importantly, she needed to protect her gemstones. Thus her feet cooperated with her. She found the chief of the army was also coming to see her.

"Princess… there is an attack…," chief of army tried to say something. Aarunya cut him short. "I know there is an attack… ask all the soldiers to quickly make a move… I'll be joining the battle… hurry up and get my horse ready." She almost yelled. "But princess you….," chief of army tried to express his wonder. But Aarunya again cut him short. "Just do as I say… don't argue."

Aarunya had learned arching very well, as this was her estate's forte. But she never had fought in a battle before. Still she decided in just one second that she'll fight for protection of her gemstones.

Then there was a big disturbance in the realm of Krishnapur. All the soldiers of Krishnapur started preparing their armours and weapons. There was a sudden and unalarmed attack in their realm, their moves had to be hasty. Chief of army loaded all the weapons on his arms and started instructing the cavalry. Krishnapur had less than fifty thousand people in their force. They were already less in number.

Realm of Krishnapur had to give an answer to the attack of Indragadh without their king and prince. Aarunya's pretty shoulders had to bear lots of responsibility all of a sudden. They had very little time to prepare their soldiers, organise their army and give an answer to the attack of Indragadh. The force of Indragadh had already started marching towards the realm of Krishnapur, and in no time they would cross the hill.

Aarunya first sent the message of war to her father with the help of a bird, then she wore her armour and she was all set to fight for her kingdom and gemstones.

Soon the army was all set outside the palace. Aarunya and chief of army ride on their horses. Aarunya yelled, 'Fight till your last breath! You need to protect your kingdom!" Her voice had a proclamation that she'll be leading the war in the absence of her father and brother. It was kind of demotivating for the soldiers, as they were lead by a girl of seventeen. But no one was having another option. With fear of death in their hearts and loyalty for the realm, soldiers marched.

Chief of army of realm of Krishnapur wisely sent around five thousand soldiers towards the riverside and took rest of army towards the top. He had predictions that realm of Indragadh would have sent troops to come to the palace from river's side. They were masters in archery and accordingly they had set their archers in the first two lines. On river side, more men of Krishnapur were deployed.

When the army of Krishnapur started marching up to the hill, they saw army of Indragadh had already crossed half of the hill. Those soldiers were yelling, 'Attack…Attack…Attack." The fact that they had already crossed half the hill was enough to run shiver in Krishnapur's soldier's spine. Then their cry of 'Attack' made them shiver more. But they needed to fight for their kingdom, they couldn't bear fear at that moment. Their legs started climbing the hill hastily. Aarunya roared, 'Attack! Attack! Attack!'. She did so to cheer up her army. She behaved like a perfect leader, like her father.

While the force of Krishnapur was climbing the hill, the force of Indragadh was coming down the hill. Thus, as per the natural law of physics, the speed of soldiers of Indragadh was higher than the soldiers of Krishnapur. Both armies were coming closer to each other every second. With every passing second fear of death was increasing in every soldier's hearts.

The two armies then met with a bang. Every soldier from both sides, attacked like a hungry wolf on the other side. Arrows from Indragadh started attacking the troop of Krishnapur. The soldiers from the realm of Krishnapur answered effortlessly. They were less in number but good in archery, thus they were answering better than the archers of the realm of Indragadh.

Aarunya too was arching proficiently in the battlefield. Archers of Krishnapur were confidently killing the first line of archers of the realm of Indragadh. Looking at the performance of archers, Agastya shivered about the war's consequences. They were about to lose their first line. Arrows from Aarunya and their chief of army were also brutally killing the men of Indragadh. But Agastya was still confident on his plan of sending archers first. The unalarmed attack would obviously did not give much time of preparation to the soldiers of Krishnapur. Sitting on his chariot, Agastya was waiting for the third line to come in action. This was because from the third line swordsman were performing, and soldiers of the realm of Indragadh were skilled were better swordsmen.

Agastya was deliberately moving near to the chief of the army of their kingdom. When the chief of army found that King Mahendra and Aarav weren't present in the battlefield, he looked towards Agastya. "You coward… you knew that King Mahendra and his son Aarav weren't present in the realm of Krishnapur," chief of army yelled in the middle of the battlefield. Agastya deviously looked at him.

But that wasn't the moment of argument. Chief of army concentrated on the war. Archers of Krishnapur were suppressing the archers of Indragadh. Soon the first two lines crossed and all the swordsmen too met with each other. Swords intersected each other and blood was flowing like water on the battlefield. Swordsmen of Indragadh started demonstrating their performance. Heads were decapitated like vegetables in the combat zone.

Agastya was smilingly looking at the success of his plan. Krishnapur's archers were great in arching but were less in number. Archers of Indragadh took the advantage and outnumbered archers of Indragadh survived. Soon the swordsmen of Indragadh took charge and started chopping off the heads of swordsmen of Krishnapur.

Ashoka had taken the charge to fight against the chief of the army of Krishnapur. Both of them first started fighting with the help of arrows. Ashoka was protected by his army, but the war's situation lessened the number of soldiers, who were present in his protection. Ashoka was himself master in arching, and it wasn't problematical for him to survive against one another good archer.

There Agastya was busy defending himself against the attack of archers. His war skills weren't too bad. He was able to take care of himself. His eyes were on Aarunya, and Aarunya too was fighting with her skills. She was not only defending herself but was also killing soldiers of Indragadh from her arrows. Being a girl, she was good enough on the battlefield.

There on the riverside, river Sarita's water had turned red by the blood of men from both sides. Arching wasn't possible at the riverside and this is because Indragadh's side was proving to be more powerful. Realm of Krishnapur could only send five thousand men to the riverside. Indragadh on the other side had sent more than seven thousand men to take charge of riverside. Easily Indragadh's swordsmen managed to decapitate the heads of soldiers of Krishnapur. Those soldiers were supposed to march towards the moated castle of Krishnapur.

Fighting on the hill was difficult. Chariots and horses weren't comfortable. Soon it was clearly visible that the realm of Indragadh was taking over the realm of Krishnapur. Agastya's plan was successful. Archers of Indragadh sacrificed their lives to lessen the effect of good arching of Krishnapur, and then swordsmen of Indragadh took charge very well.

While fighting, Aarunya came near the chief of the army of Indragadh. Seeing that a devious smile came on the face of Agastya. He might have wanted the same. His eyes now were both on the war and on Aarunya and chief of the army of his own realm.

Chief of the army of Indragadh was first reluctant to fight against a lady, but then survival's need persuaded him to attack. First, they tried to defeat each other with the help of arrows. Both were perfectly fine in that. None among them could defeat one other. Meanwhile, King Ashoka beheaded chief of the army of Krishnapur. He then moved towards the riverside. He soon wanted to enter in the castle of Krishnapur. When he saw Aarunya in the battlefield, his quest to bring a warrior girl in his bed increased more. Somewhere he was scared too that what if Aarunya died in the war. His purpose of leading a war would fail.

When Aarunya and chief of army ran short of arrows, they left their chariots and started fighting against each other with the help of swords. Two swords intersected each other, and a crafty battle started between the two. Aarunya was good enough but wasn't capable of defeating chief of the army of Indragadh. His sword attacked on her left arm. But to the surprise of both Aarunya and chief of the army, he couldn't hurt her. The first time he ignored. But then every time he attacked her, he wasn't able to hurt her. Blood came from her body but healed within seconds. At first, Aarunya too didn't notice her new supernatural power.

That was certainly the effect of dark magic that old lady had performed on her. She had completed the ritual by killing her mother and consequently she might have become immortal. Soul of the chief of army shivered from its core when he discovered that no matter how good he is in playing the sword, he won't be able to hurt Aarunya. He was fighting on the ground; from there he gave a look towards Agastya who was sitting on his chariot. They both looked at each other. Agastya was deceitfully smiling. Chief of army understood that he had played his dirty games against him. But in between a war, chief of army shouldn't distract himself and look towards someone else than the person against he is fighting.

He paid for it. He couldn't look back to Aarunya. Aarunya beheaded him. Soon after that action of Aarunya, Agastya came out of his chariot with a sword in his hand. He first started fighting with Aarunya. Then while Aarunya was busy in defending herself, Agastya sprinkled some powder on her. He targeted her eyes. Aarunya immediately fell on the ground. Agastya lifted her and safely put her in the chariot. He ordered the charioteer to take Aarunya awat from the battlefield.

By then the army of Indragadh had crossed the rampart of the moated castle of Krishnapur. Chief of the army of Indragadh had guided soldiers very well. They were prepared with the wooden slides to cross the castle. When Agastya had captured Aarunya in his chariot, king Ashoka was marching in the castle.

War was over. Indragadh had taken over Krishnapur.

15

Agastya's Intentions

Chitrangna was perplexed looking at her mother. Vichitra had promised that she'll resurrect after Chitrangna kills her from the special dagger. But it didn't haappen.. She found her mother dead. "Mother…. wake up! Mother," she cried. Chitrangna looked at Mahendra. His eyes were watering. "How will she wake up!" she cried on top of her voice. Her eyes were fixed on Mahendra.

"She won't" Mahendra replied in a wobbly voice. "You both lied to me," she said. She then burst into tears. In that dark night, she was crying in her loud voice. In between the woods, Chitrangna's voice was echoing. Soon Vichitra's servants started taking care of her.

"What if father comes to know of this?" She asked while looking at Mahendra. Now Mahendra was lost in thoughts. He was wondering how would Chitrangna react when she will find out that both her parents were dead. The first thing that bothered him was that will she help him in awakening the gemstones.

Servants took Chitrangna and Vichitra's body to the palace.

When Mahendra reached back to his room, he found Aarav was awake and was waiting for him. "Father, even tonight you left in the middle of the night. Where do you go in between the nights? Certainly, to meet the queen of Ratnagadh," said Aarav. When he said so Mahendra was shocked to notice that how come he noticed them together.

"Queen Vichitra is no more. She sacrificed herself to save her and our ancestors," said king Mahendra. He was still in the trauma of demise of Vichitra. "What kind of sacrifice?" Aarav questioned. But Mahendra wasn't in the state to answer all his questions. He was lost in the grief of his love. "Tomorrow we'll be going to Krishnapur with Chitrangna. Good night," he said and slept. Aarav didn't question him anymore.

Next morning when Mahendra got up, birds delivered him the message about the attack on Krishnapur by Indragadh. He was once paralyzed after reading the message from Aarunya. Both the king and prince were absent from the realm, and an attack was made by a neighbour. In such a situation he could imagine takeover by other realm.

Aarav was still sleeping on his bed. Mahendra awakened him and informed him about the attack. He too went in shock listening how could a friendly kingdom attack them. "Cowards! Attacked in our absence," Aarav murmured. "It's not the right time to comment on them we should leave for Krishnapur as soon as possible. I have no idea how Aarunya has managed them alone," said Mahendra. "Father, we are supposed to take Chitrangna with us, are we still taking her?" Aarav asked.

"Yes...," said Mahendra and he tried to add something, but Chitrangna cut him short while entering in the room. "I won't be going with you anywhere." "Chitrangna!" Mahendra uttered her name. he then continued, "You have promised your mother that you'll be coming with me and helping me to save ancestors." He didn't have time to discuss with her, his realm was under attack.

"You are the killer of my parents. Few soldiers found my father's corpse in woods. I am sure, this has something to do with you. I would have chopped your head off, if mother wasn't your friend," said Chitrangna. Vichitra had taken a step without thinking about consequences. When Chitrangna discovered the death of her father, she figured it out that it has something to do with her mother and king Mahendra.

"Chitrangna….," Mahendra tried to convince her. "Leave my palace as soon as possible, or I'll order my men to chop both of your heads. It's my mother for whom I am leaving you both alive," she proclaimed. "I am in a hurry, right now. I'll return to convince you; how important it is to save ancestors." Said Mahendra. Chitrangna was victim of both Vichitra and Mahendra.

Then Mahendra and Aarav left for Krishnapur. They didn't have time to convince Chitrangna for saving ancestors, they were thinking to save their realm first.

In the realm of Krishnapur

After taking over Krishnapur, Ashoka and Agastya were in conversation in the palace of Krishnapur. "I offer you throne of Krishnapur. Since years, this estate is being ruled by Brahmins. I would like to continue the practice," said Ashoka. "I have no interest in taking the throne of Krishnapur," said Agastya with an expressionless face. "Then what you want. I am happy with you. I want to reward you." On this dialogue of Ashoka, Agastya smiled deviously. Ashoka couldn't depict his smile.

Soon four soldiers came and tied Ashoka in chains. Ashoka could not forsee what was happening with him. "What is this.... I am the king?" Ashoka yelled. "You were," said Agastya. Ashoka kept yelling, I am the king ..... I am the king...., and soldiers dragged him and imprissioned him.

One soldier came and informed that prince Aarav and Mahendra have arrived. Agastya was keenly waiting for him. Mahendra had insulted Agastya before twenty-five years in the same palace. In the same palace, he had opened his ponytail and pledged that he'll tie it again when he'll take revenge. Agastya was mysterious. He was a nag, yet he was living like a brahmin. His hidden motives for gemstones were altogether different, and this revenge was different. Agastya ordered soldiers to bring them as prisoners in front of the king.

Soon a troop of soldiers from the realm of Indragadh made Mahendra and Aarav as prisoners and bought them in front of Agastya. Aarav and Mahendra's hand were tied in chains. When Mahendra's eyes met with Agastya's eyes, twenty-five years' older incident flashbacked in front of his eyes. He couldn't believe how come Agastya didn't age in all these years.

"Agastya," Mahendra murmured his name. While looking at him, Agastya tied his ponytail. Agastya then proceeded near Mahendra, who was standing in chains at quite a distance from the throne. Mahendra and Agastya did not take their eyes off from each other. Then after coming next to Mahendra, Agastya murmured in his ears, "Thank you for helping me by making Chitrangna a witch... and yes I have stolen that book's pages. I know how to awaken the gemstones.... But as long as I am alive, ancestors will never be saved."

Then Aarav and Mahendra were sent into cells. Mahendra's shocked eyes were gawking Agastya while he was dragged by soldiers towards the cell. Agastya too didn't take off his eyes from him.

A bird came and sat on the shoulder of Agastya. He read the message bought by the bird. 'Sahrindri and Vishnu have reached Dwarka.' Agastya had won over four realms by different tricks. Realm of Krishnapur and Indragadh were already under him. King and queen of Ratangadh already died. Chitrangna was made witch and her transformation into a witch was in Agastya's interest. Sahrindri and Vishnu absconded to Dwarka because Agastya allowed them to flee.

Standing next to the throne of Krishnapur and being the new king of Indragadh and Krishnapur, Agastya proclaimed, "***It's my era now.***

Sakshi Pareek

Sakshi Pareek took a pen in her hands in her childhood. In her school life, she was always the literary head of her school magazine. The motivation of her school's principal and English teacher allowed her to pen over hundred poems in her school's days.

She wrote her first book in the twelfth standard. Being a commerce student and following the stereotypes of society, she started pursuing a Chartered Accountancy course. She cleared the first two stages of the professional course in the first shot. But, because her inclination was writing and her passion was to become a storyteller, she left the course in between and made her way into the literary world.

Without a quest of getting recognized, earn, and get published, she penned nine books one after another. She loved switching genres of her books. To meet her expenses and become financially independent, she began working as a content writer. She is an active professional content writer working for a reputed organisation today.

She loves interacting with new people.

Find her at: Instagram: Sakshipareek.01

www.ingramcontent.com/pod-product-compliance
Lightning Source LLC
LaVergne TN
LVHW041216150826
845673LV00001B/429

* 9 7 8 9 3 9 0 5 6 7 4 4 7 *